The Anvy

Pádraig Standún

Cló Iar-Chonnachta Teo.,
Indreabhán, Conamara, Éire.

To order additional copies of this book, contact:
Bookwhip
1-855-339-3589
https://www.bookwhip.com

To all free spirits

M ammy, Mammy, Mammy!" Sarah ran to the door when she heard
Sibeál's shout from a distance. She was sure the child had fallen
into the well. But Sibeál had Patricia in her arms, alive and as well
as she could be while being carried at speed by her sister. Sibeál ran
headlong into her mother, who folded both of her children in a big hug.

"Mammy, Mammy ..." Excited and out of breath, the child could
hardly speak.

"What is it, Sibeál?" Sarah dropped to her knees, still enveloping
both children in her arms, a kind of unconscious getting down to the
child's level.

"Mammy, we saw the Anvy."

"You saw what?"

"Me and Patricia saw the Anvy."

"Patricia and ..." It was not the time or place for corrections. Sarah
tried another tack.

"You're joking me. Where?"

"Down at Tobar Ghobnatan. He was drinking in the well."

"What did I say about the well?" Sibéal was too excited to listen.

"He had hair everywhere on him."

"It was an old goat or something you saw." Sarah tried to laugh the
matter off. "Had he horns?"

"His hair was sticking out all over his head and face."

"Did he frighten you?"

"He didn't, Mammy." Sibéal pressed even closer to her mother. "He
did, a bit, but he was nice at the same time."

"How do you mean he was nice?"

"He talked nice, like."

"He talked to you?" Sarah seemed astounded.

"He can talk the same as anyone."

"And what did he say?"

"He asked whose we were, what family we were from."

"And what did you say?"

"I said that Mammy and Daddy said not to be talking to strangers."

"Good girl." Sarah hugged her closely. "And what had he to say to that?"

"He started laughing and then he took a lep over the wall."

"Are you sure it wasn't some old man acting the eejit?"

"He had no clothes at all on him." Sibéal gave a little giggle. "You could see his willy hanging down."

"Was Patricia frightened?" Sarah didn't know whether it was better to pursue the 'willy' angle or not, wondering was there a flasher on the island. She thought it better not to emphasise that aspect, for the moment at least.

"Patricia said 'bo-bo' like she says for every animal."

"Bo-bo," said the one year old, as if on cue, catching her mother around the neck at the same time. Sarah stood up, carrying the baby with her and led Sibéal into the house. "Come on until I make you something nice."

"Can I have crisps, Mam?"

"You can have a packet between you. I want you to have an appetite for your dinner. Your Daddy will be home in half an hour." Sarah put the children on the big soft armchair together, and switched on the cartoons on the television. Eating their crisps they seemed unconcerned about whatever it was they had seen or seemed to have seen, but Sarah was worried. There had been talk of the Anvy on the island since she was a child herself. Some kind of bogeyman idea, a cross between a pooka and a ghost, it was used to help discipline children. "Mind yourself or the Anvy will get you," helped hurry many a one home before nightfall. Nobody really believed in it, but nobody was sure either.

Sarah's own sister, Maggie, had claimed to have seen the Anvy many years before, when she was about Sibéal's age. But you could never know with Maggie. She always had a vivid imagination, and seemed to hover at times on the verge of the insanity that had her hospitalised in Ballinasloe at one stage. Maggie claimed it was their mother, now referred to as 'Mamó,' since Sarah's children were born, that drove her over the top as they used to say.

Sarah had always envied her sister's beauty but was glad to have avoided her instability. Maggie never married, and continued to care for their mother who, weakened by strokes, barely struggled from the bed to her fireside chair each day. If her sister was to be believed, the mother had lost the use of her mind as well as her feet, but the old woman was as sweet as pie to herself when she visited the old place, as she did most evenings.

Just as Sibéal had said earlier, Maggie too had found the Anvy kind and courteous, a direct contradiction of his generally held reputation to be some kind of vicious wild animal. Rumour of his presence on the island had been so rife once that the men had gone to hunt for him with guns and dogs. They had returned somewhat shamefacedly, Mártan's ram mistakenly shot by Tom Shéamais Mhaig. Some of the men swore they had seen the Anvy crossing walls four or five fields in front of them, before going over a cliff-edge into the sea. As the hunt had taken place on a Sunday afternoon when the pub closed for the so-called holy hour, the whole episode became somewhat of a joke on the island.

There were those who claimed that the Anvy was the devil himself from hell, with clubbed feet, horns and a tail. Others claimed he was some kind of guardian angel, that had helped many a cow or sheep at birth, that it was he who hauled some of the currachs to safety the night of the great storm. Many would say that the living was more dangerous than the dead, assuming the Anvy belonged to the other world. When Sarah returned to the living room from the kitchen, she found both children asleep on the couch despite the cartoons that blinked and shouted in their daft accents on the television screen. She felt her love for them well up inside her as she thought of how she would die if anything happened them. The sleep will do them good, she thought. "Maybe they often see worse on the telly than what they saw, or thought they saw this evening."

Ω Ω Ω

Maggie barely answered her mother any more. She closed her mind against her. The old woman had driven her mental once already, and she wasn't going to let it happen again. She didn't really understand why she stayed on to care for the old bitch, but what else could she do? Sometimes she felt she hated more than loved her mother. But if she didn't care for her, she would be thrown into some kind of nursing home. There was no greater stigma on the island than to finish up in the county home. Anything but that.

Apart from Sarah, all the other members of the family had emigrated. Tomás, Sarah's husband, couldn't stick his mother-in-law. There was no way Mamó could stay with them, but Sarah called most evenings, something Maggie always looked forward to. Her mother always calmed down while Sarah was there. It gave Maggie a bit of a rest, and she always enjoyed their conversations. Sarah was not just her sister, but her best friend as well.

"I know well why you are trying to get rid of me," her mother said, as they slowly climbed the stairs, step by step. "That ould devil is coming around again."

"Who is coming around again?" Maggie had answered before she thought of herself, despite her intention to keep her mouth shut.

"You know as well as I do, the same one that comes every night."

"Nobody comes here every night." Maggie replied slowly, resignedly. "Sarah comes to visit most nights. Who else would put up with you?"

"Don't I hear yourself and himself skitting laughing every night after I go to bed. You can't fool me. I'm no óinseach, I'll have you know. I know well the carry-on of the two of you."

"I wish to God I was as popular as you make me out to be."

"If I had my health it's the stick the two of you would get." Kate, the old woman, raised her gnarled blackthorn. "I'd redden your whooring backsides for you." She stumbled, and almost fell with her effort. Maggie felt an almost uncontrollable urge to laugh, and almost bit her tongue to restrain herself. Ten more minutes, she thought. Ten more minutes and I'll be finished with her for today. Three more minutes on the stairs, she told herself in an effort to remain patient. About five minutes in the toilet, and into the bed then, door closed, the worst of another day done.

It wouldn't stop the shouting, the insults, the banging of the stick on the floor. But Maggie would be downstairs, her feet up, a cup of coffee in one hand, a cigarette in the other, the television on loudly with one of the evening soap operas, a whiskey punch later with Sarah when she would call, after putting her children to bed.

"I suppose it's a married man you are entertaining. That's why you don't want me to know anything about him," her mother rambled on with her usual cant. She managed to sting Maggie by her next remarks: "I'm going to tell on you. I'm going to tell the priest the next day he comes to see me."

"It's a pity you can't be half as nice to your own daughter as you are to the priest. You're sweet alright when he calls, Father this and Father that." Maggie tried to imitate her mother. "No wonder he thinks the sun, moon and stars shine out of you, his angel ... Devil more like it. If he was to hear that you don't have a civil word out of you for the one that looks after you, day and night."

"I'll tell him about you, you whooring bitch."

"Get up on that toilet there, you ould witch." Maggie's anger exploded at last. "And when you're done with that, get into bed. I don't want to hear a gig out of you before morning. I'm fed up to the teeth with your old lying shit." She banged the bathroom door, but stood outside. Despite her anger she couldn't let her mother find her own way from there. She would surely fall and Maggie would end up blaming herself. Ten more minutes, she thought, and I will have a fag in my mouth.

Maggie was thirty eight years old, tall and thin, older looking than her years because she refused to colour her greying hair. She had taken very little care of herself for a long time now, and had a downy moustache growing on her upper lip. She had not been off the island for more than three years, that time she was in the hospital. Her clothes were hand-me-downs from the much more plump Sarah, large woollen jumpers hanging loose. Maggie didn't care. "They will come into fashion sometime," she used to say.

She could hardly wait for Sarah to come. Her sister was her window to the world, lively, talkative, to a large extent uninhibited. She would think nothing of giving Maggie a running commentary on her sexlife with Tomás. Claiming, like Marlene Dietrich, that sex was an overrated pastime, Sarah would burst into a rolling gutteral laugh which would suggest that the opposite was the case. Maggie sometimes felt that she was no more than Sarah's shadow. She felt so cut off from the outside world that she sometimes wondered was she alive at all. But she felt she was alive through her sister. Sarah brought the big world to her.

"You would think you would be ashamed of yourself, you dirty whore ..." Her mother hadn't finished yet, but her voice seemed to have lost its venom. At this stage Maggie didn't care as she tucked the old woman into bed. "We're shamed to the world," the old woman muttered, almost affectionately.

Old Kate was in bed at last, her rosary beads in her hand, the holy water sprinkled, a mixture of prayer and curses gurgling from her lips. Maggie went down the stairs two at a time. Another day ...

As soon as Sarah entered the house later in the evening, Maggie knew that she had something unusual to tell. Although there was thirteen months between their ages, they were in many ways like twins. They had been in the same class at school, Maggie held back a year because of her poor health. Inseperable in their youth, they had only been apart for the few years Sarah spent in the United States before she returned to marry Tomás. They always seemed to have a telepathy between them, despite the fact that they had been treated so differently by their mother.

Since childhood Maggie had always felt that Sarah was loved more than she was. As time went by she had worked out that this had something to do with the short time between their births. When Kate had become pregnant again four months after Maggie's birth, the child had been left with her grandmother until Sarah was born. Maggie thought that deep down inside she had felt abandoned by her mother, that this had caused the rift that lay between them for the rest of their lives. Theories she heard expressed on radio programmes about the effect of one's earlier experiences on the whole of life seemed to confirm her notion. Was it not ironic, she thought, that it was to be her lot to care for her mother in her dotage?

Sarah ran upstairs almost as soon as she entered the house, to check if her mother was awake. She found her peaceful, about to drift into sleep, but alert enough to enquire after the children. "When are they coming to see their old grandmother?" she asked. "I love those little ones with all my heart."

Sarah always found it hard to believe that her mother treated Maggie as badly as she claimed. She had put it down to her sister's highly strung personality until she heard the old woman mutter words like whore, cunt, and bitch from time to time.

"She has settled," Sarah said in a loud whisper as she closed the door to the narrow stairway that led up from the kitchen.

"A pity I haven't your touch," Maggie replied.

"Only for you she would be in a right mess altogether," her sister reassured her. "Too bad she doesn't recognise or appreciate it."

"We might all be the same when we are that age." Having had time to herself after getting her mother to bed, Maggie felt better now. "Most days I can let it in one ear and out the other, but she drives me past breaking point some days. I nearly lost the head tonight, couldn't put up with any more of her old *seafóid*."

"What was she on about this time?"

"The usual, but it's easier to take some days than others." Maggie had tea made and they settled in their usual armchairs. "Anyway that's enough about me. What is it that you're bursting to tell me?"

"Is it that obvious?" Sarah smiled, but quickly became serious, worried still about what had been seen at the well. "Didn't the children come home this evening saying they saw the Anvy."

"At Tobar Ghobnatan, I suppose? Well, I hope you believed them."

"You can't say it is an easy thing to believe. You would hear talk of people seeing things at night. But in broad daylight, so near to the houses... And it's not the first fib Sibéal told."

"Didn't you say the children?"

"Patricia is hardly a first-class witness. All she said was bo-bo."

"I saw him myself," Maggie said, "as clearly as I see you now. I don't think that there is a bit of harm in him."

"But what is he? Who is he? Where did he come from? Is he human, or what?"

"Don't ask me. All I know is that he exists, that the Anvy is real. I saw him."

"People see statues moving too. People see all sorts of things."

"I think it's a bad thing not to believe children. They are not often believed either when they are being abused."

"You know as well as I do," Sarah said curtly, "that my children are not being abused."

"That's not what I'm saying, just not to dismiss what they say about the Anvy. Anyway I don't think he is something bad.'

"Funny enough that's what Sibéal said too, that there was something nice about him. I never thought of him as something real, just some kind of *púca* or bogeyman, made up to frighten children."

"They could see worse," Maggie said. "I'm sure he's no worse than that Anvy upstairs, their own grandmother."

"Such a thing to say about your own mother." But Sarah saw the humour in it and they both had a good laugh.

"True for me," Maggie smiled. "I doubt if the Anvy spends the day insulting people and calling them names."

"I'll never forget the time," Sarah reminisced, "that we were in the city, and took Sibéal to see Jack and the Beanstalk. She had nightmares for months afterwards. She would wake up and say 'Fee, Fi, Fo, Fum' was after her. I hope it will not be the same with the Anvy."

"If she never sees worse, she will be alright," Maggie said. "When she was not scared at the time, I doubt if it's going to affect her." The sisters talked on until the small hours, their shoes kicked off, punch to drink, relaxed before the fire. Neither noticed the eye that peered through the opening between the poorly drawn curtains.

Ω Ω Ω

Blast took both sides of the road with him on his merry way home from the island public house. It was not his first time to have a few too many, and he had no doubt but that it would not be his last. As he used to say, "There's nothing in this life as good as a blast of porter." The lads would reply on cue, "Even better than Biddy?" This gave him the opening for what he considered his best line "Porter for the belly, woman for the bud." The' bud' in question was the Irish *bod*. You could get away with that, while the English word 'prick' might get a man barred. Blast could envisage no hell worse than being barred from the one pub in the place.

"Porter for the belly, woman for the bud," he repeated to himself as he wandered along the road. That one always got a laugh. That got the lads going. He would have to be careful though, he thought, not to let it slip out in Biddy's presence. She would kill him altogether.

Blast was not able to drink as much as he used to. Even he himself recognised that. His legs got wobbly much quicker than in the old days. Biddy had noticed that too, and she had begun to keep a much tighter rein on the purse. However she had managed it, she had got the Post Office to pay both their pensions jointly into her hand, money she dealt out most sparingly. The price of three pints was all she doled out to him at any one time.

"Doctor's orders," she emphasised, and then as if she was doing him a great favour, "In fact the doctor said no more than two pints a day, but since I'm easy-going ..." When was she ever easy-going?

Blast had tried hard to make the case that if the doctor had said two pints a day, that meant fourteen pints a week. As he only went to the pub twice weekly he argued that he should be entitled to seven pints on Friday, pension day, and seven more on Sunday, after Mass. Logic didn't seem to be one of Biddy's finer points, and she threatened to only let him out once a week if he didn't "give over," as she put it. He had thought it better to keep quiet about money matters from then on.

That did not mean, however, that he was beaten. Biddy had won the battle, but had she won the war? Blast had ways and means of expanding his liquid diet. When the tourists came around in the summer all they wanted was someone to tell about the old days. Blast was not just able to tell a story. He knew, too, how to embellish a tale and make it more interesting. And a man could hardly be expected to tell a story on a dry throat, or an empty pint glass.

Blast was not beaten in wintertime either, thanks to the European Community. He never understood why officials in Brussels and beyond sent cheques to farmers who kept sheep on the mountains and islands of Ireland. But they did, year after year. While the price of the lamb or the wool was handed over faithfully to Biddy, Blast neglected to mention the eurocheque. This was used to clear the extra few pints he put on the slate in the pub from time to time.

Biddy did not work the head on him completely with regard to the pension either. Blast had his own little revenge on account of the tightness of her purse-strings. On Fridays she sent for a bottle of whiskey for her own medicinal purposes. She wouldn't be seen dead in a pub herself. Because he had a weekly standing order Blast got the bottle a couple of pounds cheaper than the price on the label. This too represented an extra pint on pension day.

It had been a great evening. Three men had come over from the other island looking for a ram. Their search had been confined to the pub. "We are only making enquiries today," Mike Kit had said. "We'll be buying the next day." How could a man be expected to go home while stories and porter flowed? "Biddy will kill me," he told himself. "I'll be killed when I go home," as Tomeen Jim used say, Tomeen that had only a cat waiting for him on the hearth.

Blast could not understand how a night on which there should be a full moon could be so dark. He sheltered under a high wall as a heavy shower rained down. He seemed to have lost his bearings and wondered was it the dreaded *fóidín mearaí* that sent a man in the opposite direction to the one he wanted to go. Well, there was a cure for that. Turn your jacket inside out. Blast had one sleeve pulled through when the jacket fell from him and got soaked in a pool of water. Biddy would kill him, he thought, and not without reason.

Blast began to panic. The shower had passed. He could see stars above him, but absolute darkness when he looked about. Why could he not see the light of any house? It couldn't be that late, he thought. Had he lost his sight? How could he see the stars? He moved along the wall, feeling with his fingers. It felt as if he were locked into a little field with no escape.

Would he be found in the morning, dead from cold and exposure, death without absolution or anointing, he wondered? That was likely if he remained where he was. An even worse fate might await him, he thought, if he got back on the road and couldn't find his way. He could easily wander over a rock outcrop, fall into the sea. "Biddy, a *stóirín*, Biddy, a *chroí*," he found himself murmuring. "It's not killed when I go home I'll be, but killed on the way."

Then someone gently caught hold of his shoulder and, holding him at arm's length, guided him on his way. When they emerged into the moonlight Blast understood where he had gone wrong. He had wandered into an old barn with the roof partly fallen in. This explained the darkness as well as the stars and his inability to claw his way out. He tried to look at the person leading him, but the strong arm kept him sufficiently in front to prevent him seeing his helper. Whoever it was, human or otherwise, Blast thought, he, or could it be she, certainly knew the way.

When they had got to within fifty yards of his house Blast thought it would be no harm to talk, to thank his helper, and try and prevent him telling Biddy what had happened.

"I don't know how I'm going to thank you, whoever you are. Good man yourself. I'd never have got home without you." Every time Blast tried to look around, the other's arm strengthened to prevent him looking back. "You won't be telling Biddy. Not a word. Good on you. You're not one that has much to say, anway, whoever you are. Unless you're the priest. I beg your pardon, Father ..." Blast tried to raise his cap, only to find that he had lost it. He doubted that the priest could be that strong. There was no way he was going to get a glance at the mysterious figure that had helped him.

"I wonder what it was came over me," Blast mused. "It's many the blast of porter I threw back in my time, but nothing like that ever happened me. Only for yourself ... You wouldn't be the Anvy by any chance?" He got a sudden kick in the behind. By the time Blast had got over the pain and looked around, the person or thing that had led him home had disappeared.

He had intended not to tell Biddy anything in case she would never let him out again. But it was not often something miraculous happened a man, and Blast could never resist a good story. The more he played down the drink, the more Biddy blamed it, but she seemed to be glad he was home safely, despite losing his cap and having his jacket wet and dirty.

"Down to bed there with you, and keep that ould *seafóid* talk about being taken by the fairies for the Yanks in the summer. I don't know about letting you out to the pub at all again. I'll have to ask the advice of the priest."

"Whatever you do, don't do that. He's down enough on the drink as he is."

Ω Ω Ω

The priest on the island, George Gibbons, really enjoyed the company and conversation of his Mass servers. They seemed to be the least inhibited of his parishioners, and talked to him nearly as if he was one of themselves. After many years teaching in the diocesan minor seminary, the change to the island had been a new lease of life to him. The first thing he had noticed was that the place was not at all like its reputation among his fellow clergy. The time that life on an island was the most difficult assignment for a priest had passed. There had been many changes over the years, most of them for the better, though the twin evils, as he saw them, of unemployment and emigration still existed.

Electric power had brought about enormous change, giving the island people the same modern conveniences as people anywhere in the world, washing machines, fridges, freezers, television, videos. The houses of the younger couples, especially, had all of these, most having telephones as well. Insularity was no longer what it used to be.

The modern convenience which pleased the priest most was the freezer. He enjoyed cooking, and used it as pastime. He had a freezer full of meat, fish, bread, milk, and vegetables for the times those in his own garden were scarce. He had heard many tales of island priests frying up Spam to put a taste on it when fresh meat was not available due to inclement weather. That day had long gone.

George Gibbons wondered was it his many years teaching teenage boys that helped him get on so well with the servers. Sometimes they almost forgot to light the candles, they were so full of stories or the latest match they saw on television.

"Do you believe in the Anvy?" Jason Thomas asked him before Saturday night Mass. As this was the first Mass for Sunday in the new dispensation, the priest's mind was more on his sermon than on the small talk of the boys.

"The Anvy?" he had heard rumours of this strange being during his year on the island.

"You know ... Everyone knows about the Anvy," Trevor John said.

"I'm not in the place as long as everyone." The priest kicked for touch, to find out what the boys views on this thing were.

"A strange sort of a kind of an animal," was Trevor's meaning.

"Sibéilín Sarah saw it the last day." There was a hint of envy in Jason's voice.

"I'd give anything to see it."

"Why, Trevor?" the priest asked.

"Just for the crack. I'd beat the shit ..." He stopped suddenly, his face beginning to redden. The priest pretended not to notice. "Why would you want to hurt anything?"

"It's no harm to beat an animal." Jason came to his friend's defense.

"Doesn't a beating hurt?"

"You have to hurt an animal sometimes."

"Why, Jason?"

"If you had an ass, would you hit it?"

"I would not." George Gibbons was enjoying the argument. "I wouldn't want to have a sore ass," he said, feeling his backside through his vestments. The boys had a great laugh at him. "A real ass, a donkey," Trevor said. "If he was standing in the bog and he wouldn't move for you?"

"I wouldn't beat him anyway."

"How would you get him to move?"

"I'd talk nice to him. Yup, Neddy, I'd say."

"That wouldn't do a bit of good." The boys acted as if they were disgusted with his answer. "It's often harder to move Mass-servers than asses," the priest quipped, as he checked his watch. "What about the bell, the candles, the microphone?" The servers hurried to their tasks.

George Gibbons tried to remember the main points of his sermon, only to be interrupted again seconds before Mass was due to start.

"Will you come with us tomorrow after Mass, to search for the Anvy?"

"Ask me when this Mass is over. Now hands together. No whispering or laughing on the altar. Line up now and bow to the cross. Forget about the Anvy, and concentrate on the Holy Mass."

Not for the first time Father Gibbons aimed his sermon at what he called the demon drink. A recent article he had read was full of statistics about broken homes, broken marriages, traffic accidents, violence, and child abuse caused by immoderate drinking. He seemed to overlook the fact that there was no evidence of a major problem on the island in any of these areas. But he was pleased with himself. He always knew when people listened.

No sooner were they back in the sacristy after Mass than the boys were asking about the Anvy again. He promised them an answer when the candles were quenched, the altar readied for the following day's Mass and their surplices and soutanes hanging up neatly.

"My Daddy says he lives in a cave down at Trá na gCapall. That's what people say anyhow," Trevor said.

"If people know where he is, why was he not found long ago?" the priest asked.

"People went after him before, but he escaped." Jason assured him.

"Maybe people are afraid to go near that place."

"They are not, Father." Trevor answered. "It's just that they are not bothered about him. We wouldn't be let go without a grown-up. Come with us, please."

"Is this animal dangerous? Will I need a gun?" asked George Gibbons, tongue in cheek.

"Sibéal said he was nice."

"I didn't know you had a gun." Jason's voice showed his wonder.

"I don't either. I'm not that much of a cowboy, but I suppose I could borrow one. The best thing is to be ready to run if he comes after us."

Ω Ω Ω

It was often joked on the island that God saw more smoke than prayer on a Sunday morning. The old men gathered at the church gates to smoke their pipes and discuss current affairs in both the island and the wider world.

"There's no better man than yourself, Blast, to make up a story," Tomeen Rua commented. "Do you know lads what he was telling me before Mass started? That his guardian angel led him home the last night, when he stood on the *fóidín mearaí* or something like it. That's one you should keep for the pub, not for the chapel gate. They would believe there what they won't believe here."

"Believe what you want to believe," Blast said, "but I was sure the same night that I was finished. And I was too, only for I was taken by the hand ..."

"Why do people only see things on their way from the pub?" Daneen Shéamais asked the logical question. His legs half crippled from tuberculosis, Daneen was a newcomer to the gate, having only recently graduated from a disability pension to the old-age one.

"Everyone blames drink for everything," Blast answered, "even his reverence." He lowered his tone slightly in case the same reverence might be somewhere around the church door. "But it's many's the blast of porter I had since I was twelve years old, and nothing like that kind of *mearbhall* ever came on me before."

"Maybe it was the Anvy," Tomeen said. "Isn't it said that Sarah Kate's little girl saw him the other day, maybe the same day ..." Bartley Mór spoke for the first time that morning.

"There isn't a year that there is not talk of the same Anvy around this time," Tomeen said between two tobacco spits. "He is forgotten about again as soon as a few tourists come around. I think it's how people have nothing else to talk about."

"Maybe he's the kind of thing that comes around at a certain time of the year." Daneen offered another opinion. "Like the cuckoo, or the swallows."

"Maybe it's on his holidays he comes," Blast said, "like all the strangers."

"Sure it's all an ould pishrogue," Tomeen said, relighting his pipe.

"What took me home was as real as anything," Blast emphasised.

"But did he talk at all?" Bartley queried. "Not a word."

"He spoke to Sibéilín," said Daneen. "Why would he talk to one and not to another?"

"Maybe his tongue is not as long as yours, Daneen," Blast said sourly.

"Didn't Biddy say one time that your tongue was the longest part of yourself, Blast," Daneen struck back with his own bit of venom. Blast's answer was cruel:

"What would a lame old bachelor like yourself know about the long or the short of anything?" Daneen limped away slowly, his feelings obviously hurt.

"You were a bit hard on poor old Daneen, Blast." Bartley Mór was the first to speak.

"The same Daneen has a lot of poison in him." Bartley thought it time to change the subject. "And did Biddy see the Anvy, Blast?" Blast winked at Tomeen:

"Of course she did, and often."

"And what did she think?"

"She said she never saw the likes of it, that there wasn't a beginning or an end to it."

"There's no end to your tongue anyway, Blast," Tomeen said. "Daneen was right about that much anyway."

"Isn't it about time the place beyond opened." Blast nodded his head towards the pub.

Ω   Ω   Ω

George Gibbins, the priest, had barely finished his lunch when Jason and Trevor were at the door, waiting for him to join them in searching for the Anvy. They were full of excitement, sure that this was the day they were to see the strange sight. The eleven year old boys skipped along merrily, beside the priest most of the time, edging in front from time to time, as if to encourage him to hurry up.

They talked of the latest rounds of sports fixtures in hurling, gaelic football and soccer. The boys astound the priest with their in-depth knowledge, not just of English League Football, but the Italian League as well, which they assured him was the best in the world. Availability of television channels had really brought the Global Village closer, Gibbons thought, when boys from an Irish Atlantic Island talked knowingly of Milan, Juventus and Sampdoria.

The servers seemed to be experts, too, in the worlds of soap opera, particularly the Australian and American ones. Having so much free time on his hands since coming to the island, George Gibbons too had become what he described to his friends as a serial T. V. fanatic rather than a serial killer. His own favourite after the Irish produced *Glenroe* and *Fair City* was the long running Manchester series, *Coronation Street*, but he had a working knowledge of everything that moved on the small screen, particularly on the Irish channels.

Trevor expressed a disgust at what he called the kissing programmes.

"Why do you watch them so?" inquired the priest.

"There's lots of action in them as well."

What a difference in a couple of generations George Gibbons thought, as he trudged on, slightly behind the boys at this stage, as they picked their teams for the lunchtime game in the schoolyard on the following day. With only about twenty pupils to choose from, boys and girls of all ages got places on their teams. Even first names had undergone a dramatic change, Gibbons thought, Trevors, Jasons, Sharons, replacing Cóilíns, Bartleys, Máires, Mairéads.

Was it some kind of snobbery? A break with times of poverty? Did it matter? They were lovely children, whatever they were called.

"Wouldn't it be great to catch the buck." Trevor had waited for him to catch up.

"The buck?" The priest pleaded ignorance, remembering with amusement an old colleague of his own who never called the bishop anything but 'the buck.'

"The Anvy. We're not far from Trá na gCapall now. We'll show you where he has his cave." Trá na gCapall was like a natural amphitheatre, a great semicircle of a storm-beach with rocks, rounded by constant rolling in the tide, rising up to a height of thirty or forty feet above low-water level. Great rolling waves washed in slowly, each backwash drawing a low thunderous noise from the rolling stones it disturbed.

"There's a sea in it today, Father." Jason stood on top of the storm-beach, his hair blowing in the wind.

"Isn't there a sea in it every day?"

"It's calm some days. There's no sea at all in it. We only call it a sea when it's wild, when the waves are breaking in big like that."

"I'll never understand these things," the priest said, "but then I suppose a born landlubber isn't supposed to. Anyway, it's a most beautiful place."

"Three men drowned here once," Trevor said, as if he thought the priest might get too romantic about Trá na gCapall. "Come on down the far side until you see the cave." He put a cautionary finger to his lips, and George Gibbons, following with a crouch was reminded of games of cowboys and Indians forty years earlier.

"We don't even know what we are searching for," he said, as the rocks slithered beneath him, while the boys skipped over them like kid goats. "How are we going to recognise him?"

"He will be like a strange animal that you never saw the likes of in a book or on the telly." Jason seemed sure of what he was looking for.

"A kind of a goat, with a man's head on him, and a cow's horns sticking out of it," was Trevor's version of the Anvy.

"I haven't a clue what we are looking for."

"Don't worry, Father." Jason thought the adult might be getting cold feet. "We'll recognise him when we see him."

"Say a prayer if you want to," was Trevor's answer to the priest's perceived fear.

They followed each other along the base of what was like an inland cliff, where huge lumps of limestone had fallen down over millions of years perhaps. George Gibbons couldn't fail to be captured by the magic of the place, pillars of free-standing rock, overhanging cliffs, the boys slipping from outcrop to outcrop like you would see soldiers in a film. Unknown to himself, almost, he was being drawn into their game. A black hole at the base of one of the cliffs was the cave associated with the Anvy.

"Will you go in first, Father?" Jason did not seem to be as courageous as he had been earlier. "You said in the sacristy that you wanted to go in first." Trevor reminded him.

"It's good manners to let the priest go first."

"Don't worry about manners when you are on a dangerous hunt like this." Gibbons was enjoying their discomfiture. He had no notion of going into any cave or of letting children go either. "Are you sure we are in the right place?"

"This is it alright." Trevor bent down to peer into the darkness.

"Well what is the first thing a good Indian scout would do?" the priest asked.

"Look for footprints," Jason replied. "Well ... Where are they?"

"Maybe he goes in with a kind of a jump," was Trevor's theory.

Jason stepped lightly from stone to stone, to show it was possible to approach the cave without leaving any footprint.

"I can well understand why your parents would not allow you down here without an adult with you," George Gibbons said. "Anvy or no Anvy this is a very dangerous place. Only trained potholers with ropes and torches should ever go into a place like that. Most of it is probably below sea-level. You would probably go straight down into a big pool of water."

"If it was full of water the Anvy would be drowned."

"Maybe he can swim, Trevor. Anyway, I'm not going back to your parents to tell them I let you go into a big black hole like that."

"But wouldn't you be with us," went Trevor's logic.

"I wouldn't get in there for silver or gold."

The priest looked at his watch. "If I remember correctly the three of us are expected at the church for rosary and benediction at six." He tried to relieve their disappointment by promising to bring them to the Ailwee caves in the Burren in North Clare on the server's outing. "There are lights in there and you will see what the inside of a cave is really like, big holes and pools of water. And bones," he said melodramatically, "bones of a bear."

"Or of an Anvy, maybe," Trevor said.

"You could well be right. I never thought of that. Maybe the Anvy is some kind of a bear." George Gibbons had little doubt as he walked home that their story the following day at school would be that they would have found the Anvy only for the priest was too afraid to enter the cave.

Ω Ω Ω

At the bottom of the inland cliff-face beside the Community Centre, Edward Jack and Teresa Shéamaisín had their arms around each other. The music could be heard loudly on the clear night air as they cuddled and kissed. As discos go this was no great shakes. A large tape recorder stood in the corner of the hall.

Someone changed a tape from time to time. There were few young people around at that time of year. Only for the fact that many middle aged married people came out to dance, it would be hardly worth their while to open the hall at all.

"Stop will you," Teresa said, as Edward put his tongue around and around one of her nipples.

"You don't really want me to stop, do you?" He moved his tongue to her other breast.

"How do you know?"

"I know well." He kissed her on the mouth. Their tongues entwined. Teresa hung onto the much taller Edward, her arms around his neck. She wound her legs around him, feeling his erection through both pairs of jeans. "Do you really want to stop?" He fumbled with her belt, but she grabbed his hand. He moved his hand to her breasts, kneading them gently. Her body rocked against him. She flicked her tongue in his ear, and then put it in his mouth, darting in and out suddenly. "You're driving me crazy," he said.

"It's nice to have a bit of a hug." Teresa slid her feet back down to the ground.

"Some hug," Edward said moving his hand around until he was feeling between Teresa's legs through her jeans, without any resistance. Slowly he opened the zip and managed to get his fingers inside her knickers, gently carressing. "Let me," he said.

"No way," but she was opening his zip, fondling.

"You didn't mind before."

"And spent three weeks worrying about it."

"There's a cure for that." He took something from his hip pocket and put it into her hand. She felt the silvery covering.

"What's that?"

"What do you think? Chewing gum? You know well."

"A rubber." She giggled. "What am I supposed to do with it?"

"Don't be acting the óinseach. Get those off you, quick ..." Edward fumbled with the condom, got it on at last, and spread his leather jacket on the ground. Teresa lay down and spread her legs for him to enter. He lowered his jeans and lay down on her.

"Am I hurting you?" He entered slowly. "No," Teresa whispered, drawing down his head to kiss him. Edward let a sudden screech, withdrew from her and jumped to his feet at the same time.

"What's wrong?"

"Some bastard is after sticking a nettle up my arse," he said, stumbling about in the darkness. "I'll kill the fucker."

"Come back here and don't be stupid." It seemed to Teresa as if Edward had suddenly gone crazy, as her knees were caught and held apart as he satisfied himself quickly and cruelly, before jumping up and disappearing. She stood up slowly, knowing from the way he had burst and she dripped that there had been no condom. She felt sick and disgusted.

"I'm going to fucking split you," she spat out the words with a venom when he came back to look for his jacket. "Yourself and your rubber." She tried to hurl herself at him, tear at his face, but he held her arms. "You're going to pay for it if I'm up the pole." Teresa pulled her hands free and went off crying into the night.

The Anvy headed back to his cave.

Ω Ω Ω

Daneen Shéamais got a pleasant surprise when he went to fertilise his potato patch on Monday morning. It looked much better than he had imagined. He felt that he must have been quite tired on Saturday when he left the field. He had felt that less than half had been covered with seaweed, but there it lay, brown and shimmering, well past the middle of the little field.

Because of his disability, Daneen managed far less seaweed in the day than most of his neighbours, but that did not worry him. The year was long. God was good. He would have as good potatoes as any of them in the autumn. Hadn't he always.

Daneen blamed Black Jack from the pub for the tuberculosis that crippled him. Jack had been the County Council ganger at the time. A hard man. It was said that he never asked a man to do what he would not do himself. The trouble was that he didn't realise other men were not as strong, or as thick, Daneen would say, as himself.

They were building the sea-wall at the time to protect the low-lying land at the North end of the island from the flooding caused by very high springtides. For three days in a row Daneen had to stand in knee-deep water, at a time when wellington boots and waders were something worn only by rich fisherfolk. His knees had weakened after that and Daneen had spent some years in the sanatorium. He had never forgiven Black Jack, never entered his pub, though he occasionally sent one of the children from the village to get him a tin-can of porter.

Daneen carried less seaweed than other men in the creels that straddled his donkey's back. That was because he needed to be carried himself, sitting side-saddle on the rump behind the big baskets. He was in no rush. He was not in competition with anyone.

It was a good year for seaweed. The big storms that came after Christmas had piled it up on the shore. Daneen felt that there were people all over the world who would give anything to be able to fertilise the earth in such a natural, clean, and cheap way. He knew all about environmental concerns and the dangers of chemicals, from listening to his walkman radio. The same radio was the joy of his life, the earphones in his ears as the donkey made his slow way down to the shore and back again. It was his cousin, who taught in the city, who had sent him the radio. It had given him a new lease of life. Before that he used carry the big black transistor radio with him, but it was awkward. The sound always put the donkey braying, so Daneen had been confined to using it to listen to the news at lunchtime, or when he was working well away from the donkey.

He had no doubt but that people laughed and joked among themselves about his earphones, that such radios were associated more with teenagers than with pensioners. He didn't care. A man with gammy legs had long learned to live with snide remarks, though Blast's comment the previous day outside the chapel rankled a little with him still.

Still, who could be angry on such a day? The Sun shone in a clear blue sky. Great toppling waves swung onto the shore. The birds had begun to sing again for spring. He thought of a line he had heard at Mass, "This is the day the Lord has made." As for Blast, Daneen thought, you had to put up with the likes of him. He had his own way, a hurtful, insulting way with him a lot of the time, but he was not a bad man. He had the name of being a good neighbour in time of trouble, but of course you couldn't believe the 'Our Father' out of his mouth. Daneen gave absolutely no credence to the story about his guardian angel leading him home.

Towards evening Daneen clearly marked where he finished spreading the seaweed. He put four sea-rods in a row just below the *cloch mhór*. He would know in the morning was it in his eyes it was that he seemed to be getting more done than he thought the previous evening.

Ω Ω Ω

"You think you can fool me, but you can not." Maggie's mother, Kate Jimmy, was giving out again. "I saw him at the window, the dirty, hairy thing. Not for the first time, either. No wonder you be in such a hurry to get rid of me in the evening. No wonder you spend your time dolling yourself up for him."

"I haven't bought a new stitch in four years." Maggie whirled around like a fashion model. "Every single thing I have on me came from Sarah." She had made a new resolution that morning, to try kindness out on her mother, to speak reasonably, be patient, not be sarcastic. That it was not working came as no surprise. That approach had never worked before, either.

"I never saw any of them things on Sarah, and what's the big jumper for? What are you trying to hide?"

"You will be pleased to know, mother that congratulations are in order." Maggie lifted her jumper to expose her thin waistline. "There's a bouncing baby in here, if not two. I wouldn't be a bit surprised if it's twins I have with the size of me."

"It's no wonder you're so thin and you hammering away night and day with that dirty ould devil I saw at the window."

Maggie laughed "You can't win," she said. "One thing sure, mother, you were blessed with a great imagination. It's not just that you see people that are not there and hear people that are not there, but you are able to add to that, and make up a tale or two to add to the story as well. This house is funnier than the circus."

"You can't fool me. You can not fool your own mother." Old Kate raised her stick.

"Well, who do you think my lover boy is?" Maggie gave a little twirl on the floor, as if she were dancing.

"A hairy old beardy old goat of a thing."

"Maybe you are seeing something." Having glanced up at the picture of the Sacred Heart, Maggie suddenly had a theory to explain what her mother thought she was seeing. "I'll bet the holy picture is reflecting off the window from where you are sitting." She knelt down beside her mother's chair but could not see anything unusual. She went to the window itself but there was nothing to be seen in the yard but her own old bicycle she no longer used.

"Such a thing to say about the holy picture," old Kate said.

"All I said was that its reflection or shadow, or whatever you might call it, might be shining back off the window."

"You said that that hairy old goat of a thing was Our Lord."

"I didn't say that and you know well that I didn't."

"I can tell you that he's a lot more like the devil out of hell, the looks of him." The way she spoke sent shivers up Maggie's spine. She would have to tell the doctor the next time he visited the island that her mother was having this kind of hallucination, she thought.

"I don't know how you can let that hairy old yoke go up on you every night."

Maggie's anger flashed through her, and with her face just a few inches from her mother's she said with all the venom she could muster. "A pity he wouldn't go up on yourself and fuck the living daylights out of you. That might soften your cough for you. You know as well as I do that I haven't been out with any man for the best part of twenty years. I haven't been any place because I have to take care of you. I have to clean your arse and wipe your hole as if you were a baby. It hurts me. It cuts me to the quick when you make your daft old accusations. That's why I don't answer you half the time. Why can't you be like when we were young? You wouldn't say a bad word and you would beat the one who did."

The tears began to roll down the old woman's face with the viciousness of her daughter's attack. "I'll tell Sarah," she said. "I'll tell Sarah all about you."

"Any time you like." Maggie showed her very little sympathy. "Go down and stay with your pet. Tomás wouldn't be long landing you into the home, or the mental, more likely." She put her mother up to bed about two hours earlier than usual. She knew that would change her sleep patterns, as well as resulting in a wetter, dirtier bed, but Maggie didn't care. She had had enough for the day.

"She went too far again today," Maggie told Sarah when she came to visit. "After as hard as I tried to be nice to her she nearly drove me out of my mind altogether."

"What can we do with her at all?" Sarah said. "Do you know that I often pray that she will die soon?"

"Sarah!"

"When I see what you have to put up with, and I'm so little help. I would be as well to ask for a divorce as to bring her home to Tomás.

She drives him around the bend altogether, giving out about his relations."

"We'll put up with her as long as we have to." It surprised and somehow touched Maggie to find her sister so depressed about the situation. She felt that she was not in it alone.

"When you think of it," Sarah was thinking out loud. "She could live for another forty years."

"God between us and all harm." Maggie burst out laughing.

"I always think of her as an old woman, but she's not even pension age. It's the widow's pension she still gets."

"Forty years ..." Maggie shook her head. "What is it the Bible says about the blind leading the blind? It will be the sick leading the sick, her taking care of me."

"I suppose she would be alright only for the strokes she had. I hardly ever remember her as being the full shilling, and sure you're only a year older."

"She's the only mother we'll have." Maggie sounded resigned. "We will have to put up with her as long as we have her."

"Do you know what you are Maggie? A saint." Maggie laughed:

"Not if you were to believe herself." She gestured upstairs. "All the carry-on I get up to with old hairyfella."

"Would you ever let me have the loan of him?" Sarah joked.

"Stick to the man you have."

"For all the good he does me, he's so tired every night."

"I can do without the intimate details.

You'll only make me jealous."

"Of me and Tomás?"

"He's as sound a man as you could get."

"I'll have to have a right look at him when I go home," Sarah joked.

"Would you like a hot drop?" Maggie took out the whiskey bottle.

"Isn't it a bit early?"

"Sure you might as well, since you're complaining that it's the only consolation you have."

"The other isn't all it's cracked up to be either."

Maggie handed her a drink. "Here. That will put hair on your chest."

"I'm bad enough."

"At least you have something there."

"Hair?"

"No, chests," said Maggie, laughing.

"I'll bet that's what happened the hairyfella herself sees," Sarah joked. "Someone gave him something to put hair on his chest, and it never stopped growing."

"Do you know who she said it was like the last day, but the picture of Daneen Shéamais with a beard on him?"

"Maybe Daneen ig going around as a peeping Tom at night."

"Sure you would hear the hobnailed boots a mile away."

"He might be going around barefoot." Sarah thought about it for a moment before dismissing the idea. "Somehow I doubt if Daneen knows what he has it for."

"Poor old Daneen. Maybe it was dreaming about him she was."

"Or about his brother."

"Daneen has no brother."

"He had a brother that was going out with herself," Sarah indicated the upstairs room with a nod of her head.

"How do you know?"

"Tomás told me."

"Strangers know more about us than we do ourselves."

"Tomás is not a stranger. He's my husband."

"How come I never heard about it?"

"It wasn't the kind of thing a person would boast about. Sure it all happened before we were born."

"What all happened?" asked Maggie excitedly.

"The big scandal."

"You're only having me on, Sarah."

"It must have been as good as a soap opera before they had the radio and television."

"What must have? What happened? Did she jilt Daneen's brother, or what? How does Dad come into this? Where did the other fellow go?"

"Over the cliff," Sarah said matter of factly. "He killed himself, because of our mother."

Maggie looked up at the roof with a kind of admiration. "Who would associate her with love and passion? It must have been a right scandal at the time."

"Or a big story made out of a small one, as always happens on the island," Sarah said.

"You couldn't call that a small story. And was she engaged to Daneen's brother?"

Sarah looked at her watch. "You can hear the next thrilling episode tomorrow night."

"I can like fuck." Maggie was uncharacteristically rude. "You can have another drink and tell me all the gory details. I'll have an answer for her the next time she starts her insults."

"I won't tell you anything unless you swear solemnly never to breathe a word to her about it. It might well have been that that left her the way she is."

"You know I won't Sarah. Cross my heart. It must have been an awful thing altogether if we have to be so secretive about it."

"There was nothing terrible about it, just the kind of thing that happened at a time marriages were arranged the way you would sell a heifer at a fair."

"The bargain had been made with Daneen's brother?" Maggie asked, full of curiosity.

"The marriage had been arranged for Shrove Tuesday, but didn't Dad come from the States the Christmas before, and mother fell for the Yank. There was a visiting priest doing duty for the curate that was here at the time. When they went to him early on the Tuesday morning as they used do at the time, it never occurred to the priest that she was marrying the wrong man as it were."

"Sure that kind of thing wouldn't stand up in any court."

"When you got married that time, you stayed married."

"And the other fellow went for the high jump?"

"He was never seen again."

"The poor man," Maggie said, with wonder. "Could you believe it?"

"It's amazing the changes, what is it? give or take, forty years, brings. Age and wrinkles in place of youth and beauty."

"Don't remind me."

"Anyway ..." Sarah stretched herself. "I better let you go to bed. Isn't it in the morning the priest is coming around to her with the communion?"

"That always perks her up a bit, and wouldn't it be great if the good humour was to last a whole day. Sure the same man thinks she is a walking saint."

"I think that he's not too well in the head."

"Father George?"

"The way he was going on about drink the last day. Sure everybody knew he was having a go at poor old Blast."

"He's not the worst," Maggie said. "He is always kind to me."

"Oh I see, and have you the hots for him too?"

"Sarah!" Maggie became embarrassed. "I don't like talk like that."

"Sure I was only joking."

"Don't let herself up above hear you.

Things are bad enough, without being accused of chasing the man of the cloth."

"He's not bad at all, if he would cut off that old grey beard."

"If Tomás hears you, it's more than the poor man's beard that will get cut off."

"He's alright, I suppose, but I think he blames the drink for all this talk about the Anvy. He thinks that people are seeing things."

"Some people not far from here are seeing things without any drink."

"Don't remind me of old hairyfella. It's alright for you that can stop here. I have to walk home on my own."

"Have one for the road." Maggie switched on the electric kettle. "You're in no danger as long as you have Rover with you." Sarah's dog, who was stretched in front of the fire, raised his head and gave a few slow wags with his tail.

"He wasn't much good when he was with the children the last day. Sibéal said that he just wagged his tail at whatever it was she saw."

"He mustn't have sensed any danger." Maggie was philosophical, as she handed her sister the hot whiskey.

"May it not be long until you do it again," laughed Sarah. "You'll have me as drunk as a skunk going home."

"You'll be fit for any Anvy or hairyfella after that."

"Tomás's hairyfella will do me for tonight."

"I think you are drunk."

"So long as I don't step on the *fóidín mearaí*, like Blast did."

"*Fóidín* porter, I'd say," said Maggie.

"I hear Biddy has him grounded. She's not going to let him out of her sight any more."

"Good for her. It's very dangerous going home that last bit, down by the sea. It's a wonder the County Council never put a wall in it."

"They say Biddy wouldn't let them, without money. The place is still in her name. Blast only married in there. That's how she is able to keep him under control."

"I wonder was it the Anvy brought him home?" mused Maggie.

"It was supposed to be his guardian angel at first, then the Anvy ... Could there be such a thing in it?"

"We could discuss it until morning, and we wouldn't have it proven either way."

"That's another way of saying isn't it time to be going home."

"It is not, Sarah."

"I know a hint when I see one," gurgled Sarah, slightly tipsy.

"If you are able to see hints you're alright." Maggie helped her with her coat.

"The drink is gone to my head."

"Tomás won't know what hit him." Maggie thought the drink must be gone to her own head as well. She didn't normally make remarks like that.

"I don't think there will be too much action tonight, somehow. He had a heavy day today preparing for setting the spuds." She looked at her watch. "Is that the time? I've kept you too long from your bed, Maggie."

"Not at all. I enjoyed the night. I needed to relax after the way she was herself today. I suppose it won't be long now until she begins banging the floor with her stick."

"Tell her the priest is on his way. That will keep her on good behaviour."

Sarah stood outside for a moment with her eyes closed as they said their goodbyes. That would get her accustomed to the darkness after the glare of the electric light. She seldom carried a torch, except on the blackest night. There was still more than half a moon so she felt she would have no problem on a road she knew like the back of her hand. The moonlight shone in a swathe across the sea, highlighting the white rollers as they broke on the shore. It was a beautiful night.

Sarah felt lighthearted, as well as having a lightness in her head. She had often heard men say that the alcohol only hit them when they came out from the pub into the open air. She thought she knew what they meant now. Still, it was seldom she had as much, and Maggie needed cheering up.

Her shoes echoed loudly on the road in the frosty air. She stopped when she heard the echo the first time. The night's talk came back and she shivered a little as she thought of Anvies and hairyfellas wandering around the island. She blessed herself, and listened. The only sound was the thudding of the sea. She called the dog's name and he gave her a fright when he jumped out across a wall quite close to her.

A noise some distance in front of her gave her another fright, but it was just plastic with which someone had covered a pile of sea-rods flapping in the wind. The dog went over to the heap, smelled it, raised its leg and pissed nonchalantly. Sarah could see quite clearly now, and her fear lessened as she approached the house. Still she felt an urge to go faster, and somehow the echo of her shoes sounded differently. She took off her shoes altogether and ran the last fifty yards to the back door.

She quickly closed and locked the door, and lay back against it, panting, but relieved. She began to laugh at herself, asking aloud, "What has got into me at all?"

Sarah went to the children's room first. Sibéal, as usual, had thrown the clothes off herself, and would waken up, cold, later in the night, usually an excuse to snuggle in with her mother and father. But her mother had other plans for the night. She pulled up the clothes around Sibéal and tucked her in. Without wakening, Sibéal wrapped a corner of the sheet around her thumb, put it into her mouth and sucked. Patricia was sleeping on her back. Sarah gently put her lying on her side and wrapped the blankets closer about her. She had passed the age usually associated with cot deaths, but you could never be careful enough, Sarah thought. She sprinkled holy water on the children before quietly closing the latch on the door.

Tomás lay snoring in the middle of their bed, one strong arm across his forehead, shading him from the overhead light he never quenched until she came home from her mother's. "I'll soon have you snoring from the other side of your nose," she promised his sleeping body, as she took off her clothes, went into the bathroom and had a hot shower. She ran, naked, from the bathroom to the bed and hopped in beside her husband. He murmured something and turned on his side away from her, and continued sleeping, although the snoring had stopped.

Sarah lay against him, pressing herself into his back, her arm thrown around Tomás's waist. Slowly, gently she moved her hand around and around his belly, moving lower and lower. She tickled and carressed his balls, felt his erection rise, touching his foreskin with her fingernails. Tomás came awake to an intense pleasure.

"Take your time, take your time." Sarah restrained him as he tried to reach for her. She kissed him gently on the lips, put her leg across, straddling him, as he entered her with a great thrust. She had seldom been as ready, as randy, and she moved slowly up and down, enjoying the pleasure.

"What has got into you?" Tomás asked, smiling.

"What do you think has got into me? And I'd love if it stayed in me all night." She lay flat on top of him and they kissed as they had not done for a long time.

"That's the best part of it," Tomás said, "the kissing."

"Let's forget about the other so," Sarah laughed.

"OK so." Tomás lay still for a moment, then, in a quick movement, rolled over until he was on top, Sarah's legs wrapped around him, as he thrusted firmly in and out, in and out until he began to explode inside her.

"Stay there, stay there," she said urgently as her own momentum built up to an explosive climax. They lay in each other's arms, kissing occasionally. After a while Sarah said:

"Pull up the blankets a bit. I don't want you getting a cold in your tail end anyway."

"That's the only bit of me worth taking care of, I suppose."

"No. You're handy enough at setting spuds too." She gave him a little tickle. "I love every inch of you."

"Some inches more than others?"

"I love one part best of all." This was a game they oftened played, so Tomás asked the expected question: "And what part is that then?"

"A lovely soft part of you."

"Does it get hard occasionally?"

"Very rarely."

"Tonight?"

"Your big soft heart, you ould eejit." She gave him a big smacker of a kiss.

"I love every inch of you too," Tomás said. "There's far too many inches there at the moment." Sarah rubbed her hand around her waistline. "I'm getting so fat and ugly."

"Looking for compliment time now, is it?"

"God knows I could do with a few."

"You're a great ride," he joked, immediately covering himself with the blankets as she pounded him playfully with her fists. "A pity I cannot say the same about you."

"Sure you have me worn out, and it's not your imaginary weight either."

"Say that again – imaginary weight. It's not true but I love to hear it."

"More exercise ..."

"Exercise. I ran all the way home, as the song used to say."

"That's not the kind of exercise I had in mind."

"You wouldn't be up to it."

"Try me, sometime." He changed it to "some other time" when Sarah made a sudden grab in the direction of his private parts.

"Never put off until tomorrow what you can do tonight."

"But it's tomorrow already," said Tomás, raising himself on his elbow to look at the alarm clock, "and well into tomorrow."

"And there are cows to be milked, and potatoes to be set ..." She gave an exaggerated imitation of his accent.

"It's just that I have a headache," he fought back, "and I'm not in the mood." He turned over and huddled up near the side of the bed. Sarah leaned over against him.

"I'm sorry I have been like a briar for the last while, but the old lady is driving me round the bend, the way she is treating Maggie." Tomás turned towards her:

"I haven't been in top form myself recently."

"Is there something worrying you?"

"Everything in a way."

"The two of us ...?"

"Not us, not much anyway." He gave Sarah a little kiss. "Practical things, money, bad prices for cattle, hard work with no reward. I often think we'd be better off in England or the States."

"Well, we talked about that often enough, but we didn't want to bring up the children anywhere else, with drugs and everything."

"At least there wouldn't be the pishrogues, the Anvy and all that crack."

"That's really what's worrying you, Sibéal?"

"I'd hate, I don't know ..."

"You mean you'd hate if she were to turn out like Maggie."

"I didn't say that."

"You sounded as if that's what you meant."

"Don't put words into my mouth." He turned over in a tangle of bedclothes. Sarah didn't want to let him go to sleep in a huff. She stretched her body against his back:

"Tomás?" He gave a kind of a mumble: "Huh."

"I love you."

"Aaaah."

"Tomás?" He raised himself on his elbow, half turning around. Sarah slid her hand down his stomach, down, down. "Any chance on you?" she joked, a glint in her eye.

"Is there no satisfying you?" Tomás took her in his arms.

Ω Ω Ω

Daneen Shéamais decided he would have to find out who was spreading seaweed in his potato patch unknown to him. There was absolutely no doubt about it. A considerable area had been covered the previous night, well past the sea-rods he had put down as markers. He was going to find out, he promised himself, even if it took all night. He thought of bringing someone with him, but felt it would just get people laughing at him again. Isn't it Blast that would have the fun making an *amadán* out of him. He would find out for himself.

He readied himself well for the night's watch. He put the trousers of his oilskins on over his homespun britches and wellingtons. He pulled on three pullovers with the oilskin jacket over them again. A man could sleep out in that much, he thought, without catching a cold. He put his little radio with the earphones in his pocket and pulled himself up on the donkey's rump. The donkey was a bit stubborn after his day drawing seaweed, but Daneen had a carrott in his pocket, and a *gabháil* of hay under his arm for him. His flask and sandwiches were in an old travel bag hanging from his neck.

It was frosty, the moon receding, but still giving enough light to make out where you were going. The sky was freckled with stars. Daneen thought it a pity that he did not go out oftener at night to see the beauty of the sky. But where would he be going? he thought. He had sworn to himself that he would never darken the door of Black Jack's pub. "I suppose a man could go for a walk," he told himself, "but then if you had a hard day's work spreading seaweed behind you ..." His reverie was interrupted for a moment when a tall man stood aside to let the donkey pass. Bartley Mór, he presumed, but he didn't get a right look at him, as Daneen kept his head down and didn't speak. The other said nothing either. Daneen remembered some line from somewhere about ships passing in the night.

After a while Daneen almost forgot that anyone existed except himself. The night was good, lively Irish dance music rang through his earphones, the donkey walked at a slow, steady pace. It was great to be alive and embarked on an adventure. When he reached the field Daneen tied the ass to the northerly wall, where he would be sheltered from the light but cold north wind. That wall threw a shadow from the high moon which made the donkey more difficult to see.

Daneen placed the hay in front of the donkey, keeping the carrot for later, and retired to the other end of the little field. He left the flask and sandwiches to one side, and rolled the carrier bag for use as a pillow. He lay back on a piece of flat, exposed rock, well-padded and comfortable, the extra clothing to keep him warm, the oilskins to keep out the frost and the dampness.

Sometime after midnight he got tired of listening to the radio. From then on there were only the music programmes that ran all night, with hourly breaks for the news. The same news, again and again, the same put-on accents that seemed necessary on music stations. It also occurred to Daneen that he should be listening. The ears were more important than the eyes at night-time.

He poured himself some tea from the flask, ate a sandwich, forced himself to leave the rest, although he was dying for another one. But he had a long night in front of him yet, and he would surely be hungry again later on. "Amn't I the right idiot?" he said to himself, standing up, and stretching. Still he was in no doubt but that somebody was helping him out on the quiet. The way the seaweed was spread reminded him of the way his father used do it, handful after handful, to make sure every bit of grass was covered. Daneen himself tended to be sloppier than that, just to scatter the rich weed by throwing it about, hit or miss.

The two o' clock news was on when he tried the radio again, the very same news he had heard at midnight. It was not just in his potato patch that nothing was happening, he thought. He decided to wait one more hour. If anyone was to do anything, they would have to do it soon. He didn't want to be seen going home at dawn either, the *amadán* that thought someone was fertilising his potato patch. He lay back again on the crag.

It was the asses' roar that wakened him. It took Daneen a couple of minutes to adjust to his surroundings. He heard stones topple from a wall. He didn't even get a glance at who had been there, but there was the full of a creel of seaweed in a heap in the grass. Daneen was so mad with the donkey that he ate the carrot himself, along with the sandwiches.

Ω Ω Ω

The Anvy ran hard from Daneen's field down towards Trá Mhór. Although he knew that there was no danger of poor lame Daneen catching him, he had got quite a fright. He fancied himself as king of the night. He enjoyed danger to some extent, but only when he himself was in control. He was often within a couple of yards of people without them knowing or suspecting anything, but he always had his escape route marked out. He slept in the daytime for the most part, but he was king of the night, the island his kingdom.

He knew everyone on the island by sight. Some he had known, others had grown. He did not know how long he was on the run. He had kept account of the days at first, scraping little lines on the rock wall of the cave. Days ran into months, seasons, years. What was the point of counting?

Never for a moment did he feel old, feel older than the day he escaped from life, from death, but he could see the age on others, especially the ones who had gone to school with him. Many had grown-up families, their children had families of their own, but the Anvy had remained as he was when he left life. Sometimes he did not know whether he was alive or dead. He spent much of his time underground, but he was not dead. He had left life but he lived at the same time.

He wondered sometimes if he were invisible, people would pass so close to him and not see him. He would hide in the ivy across from the church gate, listening to old men who had been his own age talk of the Anvy as if it were some kind of ghost. They talked as their fathers and grandfathers had, the same talk of weather, cattle, crops, as if they were just different people speaking with the same voices. Age had come on them unawares, like sleep.

Life had changed. People got electric light from a switch on the wall. Pipes and taps brought water into every house on the island. Little did any of them know how often the Anvy shat into the big water-tanks. They sat in the evenings looking at the flickering box in the corner, curtains carelessly drawn, never suspecting that they were being watched.

He was outside life, but he lived, underground but not buried, king of the night without being either ghost or *púca*. He had jumped to his death, but lived. It must have been one of the worst nights that ever came with wind and rain. Huge waves thundered at the base of the cliff, spray rising to the dark sky. He had jumped. He remembered going through the air as if he had stood watching himself. He remembered nothing else about it, except waking up, sore and bruised on Trá na gCapall. He had no idea how long he had been in the water. He was battered, bruised, his clothes almost completely torn off him. It was a calm morning, with the tide receding.

Knowing that men would soon be walking the shoreline searching for wrack, he had dragged himself, stumbling, falling, crawling towards the black cave. He didn't want anyone to see him. Everything he had ever tried in his life had failed. Above all love had failed him. And he hadn't even been able to kill himself. He would be a laughing stock for ever, the man the sea had failed to drown.

He felt so badly, so wounded at the time that he thought he was going to die anyway. If the battering he had got on the rocks didn't kill him, the hunger and the thirst would. Even that failed. He started to eat mussels and barnacles when the hunger pains got too great. There was a continuous stream of clear fresh water in the cave. His strength came back. His wounds healed. He had been very wary of stirring out, clawing around on the rocks of Trá na gCapall for the shellfish in the dead of night. He had remembered seeing a field of turnips Bartley Mór had grown and pitted, a couple of hundred yards from the cave. He had sneaked there one night, a great adventure at the time.

He had soon discovered that there was little danger of being seen if he kept well away from the houses. He remembered hearing voices in the early days, as if there was a search going on for his body. When they hadn't found him after nine days they had probably forgotten about him.

The Anvy had gotten bolder as time elapsed and no one discovered his hiding-place. He began to venture out at night, staying well to the North, away from the houses, walking the length of Trá Mhór, running it sometimes, he felt so lively and full of energy. He began to take vegetables from different fields, a few here, a few there so that they would not be missed. That was fine in summer and autumn, but most people gathered their crops into little sheds near the houses in winter.

The dogs were the worst when he tried to get near the houses at first. He hadn't ever really noticed that every house had one or more dogs. The barking was bad enough, but they would eat you alive if they got out after you. It had taken him a long time to think of the wild garlic, but that is what did the trick for him. No dog had ever come near him since he started to rub it on himself as well as eat it.

Getting bolder all the time, he had begun to approach not just the outhouses but the houses themselves, to peer in the windows. Strange how it seldom occurred to people to look out a window at night. He never peered unless he had his own escape route ready, but it helped relieve his loneliness to see people in their warm kitchens, or in a living-room before a blazing fire. It was not just in those rooms he looked. He watched what went on in bedrooms too. Some people had no shame, he thought. People you would think butter would melt in their mouths got up to things animals wouldn't do. He would often masturbate as he watched.

The nearest he had come to being caught was the day the men had gone to hunt for him with the guns and dogs. He had become a bit careless at the time, venturing out more and more in daylight. He remembered the roars and the bloodthirsty shouts as he crossed wall after wall not a hundred yards in front of them. It was the *loch beag* that had saved him that day. He had gone among the rushes, even gone under the water with a hollow rush in his mouth to breathe through. He didn't leave the cave in daytime for quite a while after that.

The Anvy knew that he had grown careless again of late. But when he saw the little girl at Tobar Ghobnatan with her baby sister in her arms he had felt somehow human, that he was missing out on life. He had to talk to them, to have that much human contact, knowing as well that people were unlikely to believe what children, or people like Blast, when he was drunk, said.

He had felt drawn more and more lately to the house of Kate that he had loved and lost. He knew somehow that she had not long to live. The years ran together on him. The daughter looked like her mother used to, mother like daughter and daughter like mother, until you would forget was it with mother or daughter you were in love. If he was not more careful, he thought, he would be caught, sooner or later. They would kill him as if he were a wild animal.

It was strange that it was his own brother who had come nearest of all to finding him out. He had pitied Daneen with his lame legs. He felt that he had let down Daneen more than anyone else when he had left life, but he had helped him as best he could over the years. He had done the same many times before, carried up seaweed on his back or digging a ridge of potatoes and putting them in the pit. His mistake had been to do too much, but he had felt Daneen needed more help as he got older. That bit extra had stood out, given him away.

He had taken a great chance too, he thought, with the girl down below the hall, but it was too good to miss. The real thing was so much better than what you did with your hand, what he had done the night before as he watched Kate's daughter and her husband. He felt himself harden again as he thought of those big breasts and rounded body, that animal of a husband sinking himself in her. And the second time, when she sucked his cock, and he licked... He couldn't stop himself thinking about it. He lay down in the sand, pushing and pumping and pulling until he was satisfied.

Except that he was not satisfied at all. He felt that he had sinned, let down the best friend he had, the only friend he had, God. The Anvy spent a part of most nights in God's house, the island church, which was never locked. He prayed before the little red light that denoted the tabernacle, the dwelling place of the body and blood of Christ, his Saviour. That was where the Anvy felt most at home, most understood. God and he were very great. Was it not God saved him from the sea? Was it not He saved him on land when they were after him with guns and dogs? Maybe it was God, too, that put little pleasures and consolations in his way. The girl by the hall might have been God's way of thanking him for bringing home Blast safely the other night. God's ways are not our ways, he thought.

He remembered the two women that camped on the beach, that he pleasured both of them the same night, when they came back roaring drunk from the pub. Those were the coleens that had no shame, that licked each other as well as him. He knew too what it was like when a woman took it in her mouth.

People said, priests said that sort of thing didn't please God. But how did they know? What was it but human nature? Was it not that way the person came to be, as well as the animal? What was it but the work of God, the work of the Creator?

Next to God the Anvy felt the sea was his friend. Sometimes he felt that God and the sea were one. The sea breathed, fast and slow. The waves were its pulse. The person was prone to storms as were sea and God. There was quiet and calm too, ebb and flow. The sea, the night and God were the Anvy's friends.

He often sneaked around the back of the bar long after closing time. There was never a bottle without a drop in it, the full of a spoon of whiskey at times. Beer, spirits, or wine were all the same to him. He drained them all into one bottle, and brought them back to the cave to keep the cold out of his bones. He was careful enough never to drink except in the cave before going to sleep.

He did not always sleep in the cave. It depended where he was, or what season was in it. He would sometimes sleep in the ivy near the church, sometimes in fissures in the limestone. In summer he often slept in the sandhills beside Trá Mhór, hoping for some more drunken campers. He would cover himself in sand, apart from his mouth, nose and eyes. A man had walked across him once without noticing.

It was amazing the amount a man could do in a night, walk half the island, help out someone like Daneen or Blast, help a cow calving or a sheep lambing, collect enough to eat and drink for a week, see what everyone was doing, pray for a while before God's altar. He would return to his cave, heavy with sleep, happy. The Anvy was king of the night.

Ω Ω Ω

Blast felt that he was shamed to the world. Word had got out that he was like a child, not allowed out after dark. It was alright to go for a drink after Mass on Sunday or any other day either, so long as he was home in time. Biddy had laid down the law, Biddy Hitler, Biddy Stalin, Biddy bitch. Blast couldn't think of a name bad enough for her. "What," he asked himself, "do people do when all other methods fail?" They go on strike. Blast decided to go on strike.

When Biddy turned towards him and snuggled against him after going to bed, Blast turned away from her. That particular strike didn't bring about any breakthrough in the negotiations. "Ah, get up on yourself," she said, turned over, and was soon snoring.

The second strike was bed-related too. "I'm sick," Blast said, when she told him it was time to go out and milk the cow. "You were sick many a morning before," she told him, " and it didn't take you long to find a cure." She got up and did the milking, something she hadn't done for years. To make matters worse, she had got more milk from the cow than he ever got, which gave her one more cause for complaint. He had an answer for that one alright, "Why dont you milk her yourself any more?"

Like a true Irish patriot, Blast thought the hunger strike to be his last remaining hope. He went on hunger strike, or to put it more accurately, he pretended that he was on hunger strike.

He cut himself a quick slice of brown bread while Biddy was out milking the cow. He repeated the feat any time she left the house during the day. That didn't fool Biddy. She locked the bread into the pantry, complaining that it was the worst year she ever saw for rats, "half the good cake eaten at them."

Biddy went to the shop and bought a thick slice of bacon. This she put roasting on the tongs over the hot fire. The smell permeated the whole house. "Isn't it an awful pity you had to be on hunger strike the day that's in it," she shouted back to the room to him. The Black and Tans had nothing on that ould bitch, Blast thought, when it comes to torture. But he didn't give in. He pulled the blankets up over his head, and continued his strike.

The thirst strike was worse than the hunger strike. It was not that he didn't have a mug of water at his bedside. His thirst was for something stronger. He had a bottle of poteen hidden under the bag of yellow meal in the small shed. He was watching for his chance when Biddy would go out to do the evening milking. She seemed to be in no hurry, despite his reminders.

"It's going to burst," he shouted up to the kitchen.

"You'll have the blankets destroyed."

"The cow's udder I'm talking about, you dirty thing."

"I thought you might have been milking the bull."

"That's the worst I ever heard, but talk never milked a cow,"

"If you're that worried about her, go out and milk her yourself."

"I can't. I'm on hunger strike. I'm on my last."

"Don't be acting the baby. Get up and have a bit of sense."

"The bones will soon be coming out through my skin."

"You know the cure. Get up and have your dinner. I'll even go so far as to bring your dinner to the room, if it goes to that."

"Send for the priest until I make my will."

"Sure what have you to leave?"

"I wouldn't like to put a curse on anyone by leaving you to them anyways."

"All you have to do is follow a few simple rules," Biddy said. "There would be none of this only for you made a fool of yourself last Friday night."

"One mistake and I have to suffer for the rest of my life."

"One mistake too many, and it won't happen again, because you won't be let out after dark for it to happen again."

"If that's your last word on it, I'm finished. I give up. Bring in my beads until I prepare myself to meet my maker."

"Do you think it will take me long to get another man?" Biddy joked.

"I wouldn't put it past you."

"Well, if you're not going to milk the cow, I'll have to do it myself."

No sooner was Biddy gone out than Blast was out of the bed in a flash. He pulled on his trousers and stepped without socks into his hobnailed boots. He dragged them unlaced along the floor and out to the small shed. The poteen was gone. Biddy had the upper hand again, or thought she had. But Blast felt he had nothing to lose now. He tidied himself up a bit and headed for the pub.

There was no one in the public house except Black Jack himself behind the counter, and Bartley Mór sitting by the fire. Something good happened at last, Blast felt, when Jack stood him the first pint, quoting himself, "Porter for the belly, woman for the bud."

"And what did I do to deserve this?"

"He who was lost is found." Jack quoted the Bible as best he could. "Rumour had it that you were never going to be allowed out again."

"Where did you get that idea?"

"Everybody says Biddy has you on a tight reins since the other night."

"Blast everybody, whoever is saying that. There isn't a woman in the world that would keep me in if I wanted to go out. Well, not by giving me orders, anyway. Blast the feckers anyhow, talking about a man behind his back. Where are they themselves? I don't see too many around. Maybe it's themselves that are being kept at home."

"You never said a truer word, Blast." The last thing Black Jack wanted was confrontation. "It looks as if there's nothing stirring these days except the Anvy. The latest is that he's spreading seaweed for Daneen Shéamais in the middle of the night."

"Don't let Daneen fool you with that story," Bartley said. "Didn't I see him the other night, slipping away on his ass, down towards where he's setting the potatoes. I don't know what he's playing at."

"What time of night was that?" Jack enquired.

"Ten, half-ten. I was on my way down here for a pint before closing time."

"Maybe the Anvy has got himself an ass now," said Blast. "As for Daneen, there was always a bit of insanity in that crowd."

"Aren't you related to them yourself?" Bartley said, putting his empty glass up for a refill.

"Through marriage," Blast emphasised. "All the more reason I have to believe there is a bit of insanity there."

"I wouldn't think Biddy has lost any of her marbles," was Bartley's contribution.

"Or her marvels," Jack said, handing Bartley his pint.

"She hasn't lost her tongue, whatever else," Blast joined in their joke, as he relaxed a little after having a couple of pints. Bartley brought the conversation around to the Anvy again:

"I hear the priest is the latest to go on the look out for him. At least he went as far as the cave. Isn't it a strange thing too, with all the talk about him, no one ever went into the cave to search for him."

"Things like that are best left alone," Blast said darkly. "I'm surprised with Father George."

"As far as I can see," Jack said, "he thinks it's one big joke, and I must say I'm inclined to agree with him." Blast was having none of it:

"Anything to do with the other life, the good people, angels, púcas, ghosts, that class of a thing should be left alone. If we don't interfere with them, they won't interfere with us."

"What about the badfella, ould Nick himself?" Bartley wanted to know about the biggest devil of them all.

"Leave him alone, and he'll mind his own business," was Blast's advice.

"But aren't we supposed to be his business?" Black Jack was enjoying the arguments.

"The dropeen of holy water takes good care of that fellow." Jack jokingly complimented him: "Well, Blast, whatever about the theology, you seem to be an expert on the devilology."

"It's all right for you, Blast," Bartley joked as he got ready to leave, "you'll have the Anvy to lead you home. The rest of us have to find our own ways."

"Maybe he's at home before him, taking care of Biddy." Jack tried to join in the fun.

"He's welcome to her," was Blast's curt reply. Bartley tried to relieve the sudden tension.

"I'd say the same Biddy is well able for any man."

"Why don't you go home and ride the cat, or whatever it is that old bachelors do?" Blast said contemptuously, dismissively. Bartley shuffled towards the door. Blast and Jack sat in silence for a while, one at each side of the counter. As he neared the bottom of his pint, Blast asked: "You wouldn't mind putting a pint or two on the slate until again?"

"I can give you one anyway, but I don't think there is very much left in that last headage cheque you got for the sheep." Jack took down the account book.

"A pity a few more wouldn't be born with two heads, like that one of Daneen Shéamais's long ago. We might squeeze a pint or two extra from the cheques."

"The Anvy got the blame for that too. Daneen said there was never a ram near that ewe."

"Daneen wouldn't know a ram from a gander." Blast's opinion of his neighbour hadn't improved anything.

"You're a trace over the limit, Blast." Black Jack had concluded his computations, but sure you'll have one anyway for the road if not for anything else."

"I was hoping it would be a longer road than that, Jack."

"Ye wouldn't have any thought, yourself and herself, of selling the plot of land?" Jack thought it a good time to broach the subject nearest his heart. "Now that both of you are getting the pension."

"Isn't that a coincidence now, Jack, but we were discussing that very subject over the few potatoes the other day." Blast wouldn't dare broach the subject with Biddy, who would be very quick to point out whose the land was. But there would be many a free pint in it until Jack was to find that out.

"And what did Biddy think about it?" Jack knew who was the boss in that house too.

"Biddy's considered opinion ..." Like many a storyteller, Blast liked to show his command of language. "And she didn't reach that conclusion lightly, I'll have you know, was that if we were going to sell, there would be no point in selling except to someone that had money."

"A good point."

"Between ourselves, Jack," Blast winked across the counter, "your own name was mentioned in dispatches. What with the young fellow thinking of settling down ..."

"Edward ...?" Jack burst out laughing. "That fellow has a lot of wild oats to sow yet."

"I wont say anything."

"What are you trying to tell me, Blast?" Jack was full of attention now.

"There are those that say he has set some of that wild oats that you were talking about, and that the crop has taken."

"You're having me on, Blast."

"You asked me what I knew, and I told you what I heard."

"That little strap ... I knew she was after him."

"They used to say that it takes two to tango, Jack. As poles go, I wouldn't say that Teresa is far up the pole. I met her on the road earlier on and she still has a belly on her as flat as a bad pint."

"With the surprise you gave me I forgot to top up that last one." Jack hurried to fill up and top the cream from Blast's pint.

"May it not be long until you do it again." Blast raised his glass. "To young love." It was only guesswork, but it would place Jack under a kind of compliment to him.

Ω Ω Ω

There were few evenings now that the Anvy did not spend a little time looking in the window of Kate Jimmy's, the woman he had once loved, and almost died for. She was old and feeble now, but he had grown to like her daughter, the care she took with her mother. He had seen her too remove her clothes and wash herself in a basin before the fire on cold nights. She was thin besides her shameless sister, but the Anvy liked her better.

The nightly pattern seldom changed. The young woman linked her mother up the stairs, step by slow step. She came back to the kitchen in a little while, threw off her shoes, put her feet up on a little table, smoked cigarettes and watched the picture box until her sister came. They talked and drank tea and whiskey until late. Then the fat one went home to that animal of a husband of hers to take her pleasure, while the other poor sister washed and went to bed on her own. A waste to the world. How was it, he wondered, that the people who were good got all the hard knocks in life? But that was one for God, and God's ways are not our ways.

He remembered the mother when she was young and airy, Kate of the dark eyes and lively feet, when the open-air moonlight dances were held on the *creig mhór* on summer Sunday evenings. Kate who was to marry him. Kate, who changed her mind, who changed his life. He never blamed her as much as he blamed the Yank who swept her off her feet with his smart talk and his cigars. A loud-mouthed Yank after only four years in New York.

Kate was a cripple now, he was a vagabond, she confined inside, he condemned to the outer darkness. Sometimes he wondered had he really died and gone to hell. And yet he was the one that was free, she the prisoner, she had lost and he had won. But had she lost? She had children, a couple of lovely grandchildren. All he had were the roads and windows on other people's lives.

Sometimes he wished that Kate's children were his own. At other times he was glad that they were not, because it was with the thin daughter he was in love now. She was her mother before the mother aged. She was the mother without the mother's flightiness in her youth. She was steady, strong. She would not let a man down. If only there was some way to reach her, to woo her, to win her ...

The Anvy had thought a lot lately about going back to the world, giving himself up to the priest, maybe, someone that would hardly attack and beat him. He had little doubt but that it was to the mental hospital he would be sent, to live out the rest of his days in that grim grey prison. The roads, the cave were better than that any day.

Even if he was not put away, how would Daneen take to the brother that had disappeared for half his life? The brother he had Masses offered for, year after year. How would he take to a man that seemed to come back from the dead? He would be better off to remain his own master, he thought. He could go anywhere he wanted any night. He lived life and lived outside life at the same time. No one was able to find him, to catch up with him. He was the Anvy, the king of the night.

He slipped away from the window when the fat one got up to put on her coat. He hid beside the *scioból* until she passed on her way home. He did not follow. He went in the opposite direction, down to Trá Mhór, and around the curve of that mile-long beach, across the rocks then until he came to Trá na gCapall. Down near the low tide he gathered barnacles, eating them raw, swallowing them after a quick rubbery chew. The mussels grew there in their millions, but they were too small to bother about. Once they gained any size, they were swept away by the tides. The sky in the East was beginning to brighten before he slipped into the darkness of the cave.

He was so familiar with the narrow entrance that he went through like an eel, crawled the next piece on his hands and knees and emerged in a space as big as a room, through which the well-spring of fresh water flowed. The Anvy fumbled around until he found the candles and matches he took regularly from the chapel. The light flickered onto his store of wrack from the shore, turnips, potatoes, carrots gathered in handfuls here and there, piles of emptied seashells, pieces of glass and plastic that had floated in on the tide, and created colour in his surroundings, bottles upon bottles he had brought from outside Black Jack's over the years.

He drank from one of the bottles, pulled a ragged sheepskin across himself, and went to sleep, the penny candle still flickering.

Ω Ω Ω

Edward Jack, Black Jack's son, was serving in the grocery part of the business next to the bar. A tall, bearded man in his mid-twenties, he was considered very handsome by the island women, young and old. Most people preferred to see him rather than his father in the shop. Jack seemed to have a poor memory for prices, apart from the price of pints.

Groceries tended to go up and down in cost according to the mood that he was in on the day.

Teresa Shéamaisín went into the shop early, hoping to find Edward on his own. She had not seen him since the night of the disco.

"Teresa, *a stór*," he said airily, "what can I do you for?"

"I'd like to talk to you," she said crossly. "I thought that is what you're doing."

"Privately. I would like to talk with you privately."

"I don't see anyone else."

"I hate you," Teresa said vehemently.

"Are you trying to tell me you don't love me anymore?" Edward continued to treat her anger as if it were funny.

"You know well while I'm here."

"Are you trying to tell me something?"

"I'm sure you're able to guess. Even you aren't that thick."

"You're not serious. You couldn't be serious?"

"I'm after missing my period."

"Ssssssh!" Edward turned around to check for a reaction from the kitchen, which was only separated from the shop by a wooden partition.

"Now you might take me seriously, or do you want me to tell your mother?"

"But sure it's only about a week ..."

"Well, it was due."

"But I had that thing on, I didn't even ..."

"Well, I wasn't with anyone else."

"But, it's impossible. The ... the thing was still on me when I went home."

"It's not that easy make a fool out of me." Teresa said angrily.

"How can you be so sure? Do you not have to take a test, or something?"

"It was never late before."

"Give it a few more days. It couldn't be true. It would be a miracle altogether." Teresa didn't reply, just moved among the shelves as if searching for something because Blast's wife, Biddy, had just come in.

"And how is Biddy today?" Edward was back to his salesman self. "And what can you be done for?"

"I'm in no hurry. Teresa was here before me."

"It's alright. I'm still looking ..."

"Ladies first," Edward said, "and there is no more important lady than yourself." Teresa glared at him from the other side of the shelves. "I suppose I better have a look around myself as well." Biddy moved about. Teresa took down different items, looked at them, put them back again.

"Maybe it's working here you are," Biddy said to her.

"I'm shopping actually," was the ice-cold reply.

"You're taking so long about it that I was wondering was it stacking up the shelves you were, working for himself within."

"I'm not in your way, am I?"

"You are not, dear."

"Am I blocking you from paying or something?"

"I know what it is." Biddy had a brainwave. "I'm getting in the way of young love. Forgive me for being so thick." She went to where Edward sat beside the cash desk.

"Well, what's your pleasure, Biddy?"

"A pity I wasn't fifty years younger and a fine handsome man like you to ask me that. Isn't you that's the lucky one, Teresa?" Teresa pretended that she was concentrating on what was written on the label of a tin of beans.

"I don't think any other man could take Blast's place all the same, Biddy," Edward joked.

"There isn't much wagging left in his ould tail at this stage." Her voice went from high to low in a split second. "Jamaica." She winked at Edward, "from the inside place."

"I didn't think Blast drank rum." Biddy looked at him as if he still had a lot to learn. "It's for to put in a cake."

"I wouldn't mind a slice of that cake. No wonder Blast is so great with you."

"Would you ever get it for me? Good man. I have to soak the raisins." Biddy was getting impatient. Edward went out to the bar for her purchase. "That fellow is well worth going after," Biddy said to Teresa when he was gone.

"Why don't you go after him so?" she replied sourly.

"Even the course of true love does not always run smooth," Biddy said to Edward when he returned, nodding her head towards Teresa.

"What was she saying about me?"

"It's not what she said. It's what she didn't say." Biddy left, her bottle wrapped in brown paper. "Well?" Edward shrugged his shoulders.

"You'll pay for this." Teresa almost spat at him.

"So we've come to the bottom line. Pay. Well, I wont be paying for something I didn't do."

"We'll see about that."

"The oldest trick in the book," Edward said. "Well, I wasn't with anyone else."

"I believe you," he said, sarcastically. "Thousands wouldn't."

"What does that mean?"

"Isn't it well known that you're the best ride on the island."

"You lousy bastard." Teresa took a tin of peas from the shelf and fired it at him. His football training came in useful as he managed to catch it, hurting his hand in the process. He was on to her with a smothering tackle before she could throw another tin. Teresa tried to bite his arm as he held her. Hearing the commotion, Black Jack came through from the bar.

"What's going on here?"

"Nothing." Teresa straightened her coat, and looked at him cockily. "There's nothing at all going on. Sure there isn't Edward? Answer grandad." She stalked out of the shop.

"What have you to say for yourself?" Jack asked his son.

"It's almost lunchtime," he said, looking at his watch. "Amn't I supposed to be off for an hour?" Jack felt that it was not the time or the place to probe any further.

Ω Ω Ω

Daneen Shéamais regretted scaring off whoever it was that was fertilising his potato patch. He did not help any more, and as small as the field was, Daneen never found it so big before. He had finished with the seaweed and started trenching for ridges. The work was hard because of his bad legs, but there was not the same satisfaction in it as there had been in previous years. Something was gnawing at his conscience, and he was not quite sure what it was.

It had something to do with the way the seaweed was scattered. Could his father be helping him from beyond the grave? he wondered. There used be a lot of talk of the dead coming back in days gone by, but some of the priests had mocked the idea, called it a lot of *seafóid* and pishrogues. Still, Daneen thought, if there was an after-life, and he had no doubt but that there was, there had to be room for the souls of the dead to be seen occasionally. It was a question of faith. Who better to ask for advice, except Father George?

Daneen had never set foot in a house as comfortable or as warm as the priest's. There were carpets on the floors, big soft chairs in the sitting room, a big open fire, books lining the wall from floor to roof. Father Gibbons shook his hand, seated him in a big armchair, offered him a drink. He was so welcoming that Daneen presumed he must be lonely. He accepted a bottle of porter, while he couldn't help noticing how much neat whiskey the other man put in his own glass.

"Do you be lonesome here on your own, Father?" Daneen felt the need to make conversation.

"Lonely? Not at all. Who could be lonely with all that reading to do?" He waved a hand in the direction of the bookshelves. "Not to speak of the radio and the television."

"You're not long in it yet. A lot of the priests that were here before you used to be complaining that the island was a lonely station for a priest."

"A lot of those were young fellows straight out of college, used to plenty of company. An old fellow like me likes to take life nice and easy."

"You're a bit young yet to be talking of old age, Father."

"I don't think either of us is likely to see the fifty mark again, Dan."

"True for you, and some of us won't be seeing the sixty either."

"Do you be lonely yourself?" the priest asked. "No more than myself you are on your own there without kith or kin to distract you."

"I'm never lonely when I have the radio."

"I prefer it to the television myself. That's not to say that I don't watch far too much on the TV, but the old box doesn't leave much room to the imagination. With the radio, or with reading you get to see it all with the eyes of your own mind."

"My cousin in Dublin sent me one of those radios with the little earphones you can put on your ears," Daneen said. " I bring it everywhere with me. I even have the radio on the ass when I'm going down to the potato field."

"You put the earphones on the donkey." The priest had misunderstood what he said. Daneen was wondering had the other man too much to drink.

"On my own ears while I'm sitting on the ass. Sure the other radio used to drive him crazy, he never stopped braying, once I switched it on." They both laughed at that and felt somewhat more relaxed. Daneen accepted another bottle of porter with a certain amount of trepidation, afraid that he was encouraging the priest to drink more than he should. At least he seemed very open about it, filling his whiskey nearly to the rim of an admittedly smallish glass.

"Do you believe in ghosts, Father?" The question took the priest slightly aback.

"Ghosts! Well, put it like this, I'd prefer any other company."

"You don't not believe in them so?"

"I do and I don't, I suppose. I never gave them much thought, to be honest with you. I never saw a ghost and I never want to see one. But I have an open mind on whether they can exist or not. What about yourself? Do you believe in them?"

"I don't know, Father. I'm not a man of much education. That's why I came to you about it ..." He told the full story about the seaweed, his waiting to try and catch whoever was doing it, the asses' roar, the stones falling from the wall.

"One thing sure, Dan," the priest assured him, " a ghost wouldn't be knocking a wall or carrying seaweed. I'd be inclined to believe that what you have is a good neighbour, someone that does not let his left hand know what his right hand is doing, that doesn't boast about his good works. Isn't that the best kind of ghost?"

"When you look at it like that, I suppose you are right. It wasn't harm that he was doing anyway."

"I must say that what you have just told me is one of the nicest things that I heard in a long time." George Gibbons seemed to be getting carried away with the goodness of it all. "I have heard of many a kind of charity, Dan, but for practical love of the neighbour, this is hard to beat. You'll have another bottle?"

Daneen cringed when he heard 'bottle' come from the priest's lips as 'bockle'. Other words were beginning to slur as well. Daneen refused the drink, but asked the question that had brought him there in the first place. "Do you think it could be my father that was doing it?"

"Your father is a long time dead now, Dan?" George Gibbons wanted to handle the matter sensitively, but was not sure how to approach it properly.

"Thirty seven years since Candlemas, but I would swear the mark of his hand was on the way that seaweed was spread." The priest thought Daneen might have imagined it all, but felt that he could not come out and say so. He tried another approach:

"I would imagine many's the man, and woman for that matter, has the same style of spreading seaweed."

"It's the kind of thing I would notice. I always notice something that's well done. I was never that handy myself, but I would notice the one that was. My brother now, he took after the father a lot more than I did. He would spread the seaweed in the self-same fashion, hand after hand, so that he would miss nothing."

"I didn't know you even had a brother."

"Sure I had a Mass said for him on the anniversary of the time he was drowned. Timeen was his name."

"I was new to the place and didn't know who the man was. Drowned he was?"

"The only brother I had, jumped in off the cliff ..."

"The poor man. I'm sorry to hear that."

"It's a long time ago now, give or take forty years, Father. I tried to follow him, to stop him, when he said that he was going to do it, but my legs were as bad then as they are now. By the time I called the neighbours ..." Daneen reflected: "He must have weighed himself down with stones. That's what they do when they don't want to come up again."

"Was he just suicidal, as they say, or did something spark this off?" The priest tried to probe as gently as he could, while feeling his question was still a very blunt instrument, as he tried to make sense in his mind of the seaweed story.

"It was how the woman he was to marry let him down. He went bad in the head on account of it, let it get on his nerves."

"And you didn't even have the consolation of finding the body?"

"It was just as well at the time. Those that did away with themselves weren't allowed to be buried in the graveyard." George Gibbons brooded in his own mind for a couple of minutes on the cruelties perpetrated by a supposedly caring church. He had always felt that whatever anticlericism there was, especially in the media, was well earned. Daneen interrupted his reverie. "You think it was one of the neighbours that was doing the seaweed, Father?"

"It's a strange thing Daneen, but the clergy are usually the last people to believe in supernatural goings on. We need to be very careful in those areas, because many a one was made a fool of in the past, by jumping to conclusions too quickly. The dark of the night can play strange tricks on us. Isn't it often said that it was the electric light got rid of the ghosts and the fairies from rural Ireland?"

"You wouldn't have any belief so in the Anvy?"

"A pure figment of the imagination. But don't get me wrong, I admire imagination."

"I heard you were looking for it the last day yourself."

"I went along with the lads. It was great to see their excitement, but sure how could there be the likes of that wandering about in a small island in this day and age? No, Dan, I think the only Anvy around here is this." He raised his whiskey glass.

Ω Ω Ω

Father George Gibbons didn't know where he was when the pounding started at his door in the middle of the night. He felt completely disorientated in the pitch-black room. Instead of feeling for the lightswitch beside the bed, he jumped out into the middle of the floor, and then didn't know which way to turn. He felt as if the urine was about to explode in his bladder, but couldn't find the door to go to the toilet. He clawed around frantically to find his bearings, as the banging at the door got louder and louder. He shouted "Coming" at the top of his voice just as he was accidently sweeping the bedside light from its little table. The bulb exploded as the phone clattered down on top of it.

The priest had his bearings now, knowing immediately where the room door and the wall- switch for the light were, but he was afraid to walk in that direction in case he cut his bare feet on broken glass. On hands and knees, he felt for his slippers underneath the bed, eventually found them, and shuffled towards the door in such a way that he would kick aside any broken glass he encountered. The person at the front door seemed to be very distraught and was shouting as well as beating at the timber. There was a moment's respite from the banging as the lights went on.

"I have to have a piss, or I'll burst," the priest told himself, splashing all over the toilet seat as he relieved his bursting bladder. "Dear God I'll never drink again," he promised, hoping against hope that this was not an urgent sick call that would bring him out in the middle of the frosty night. "I'm coming. Have a little bit of patience," he roared, as the pounding on the door started again. "Jesus, I'm only human," he told himself distractedly, as he took his dressing gown from the back of the bathroom door, and pulled it around himself as he went down the stairs. The door, followed by a distraught Blast, almost banged against the priest as he opened the Yale lock.

"Jesus, I thought you were dead," was Blast's greeting. He looked dishevelled, and his eyes seemed to stand out in his head.

"Is it Biddy?" George Gibbons asked, presuming that he would only be awakened in the middle of the night to go on an urgent sick call.

"Is what Biddy?" Blast looked at him incredulously.

"Is she sick? Does she need a priest?"

"Sick in the head that one is," Blast answered. Then he gave a sudden jump, grabbed hold of the priest as if trying to hide behind him. "Get them away from me," he shouted, "Get them away from me."

"What in the name of God is wrong with you? What has you so agitated? Calm down, Blast, or you'll give yourself a heart attack."

"Keep them away. Keep them away from me."

"Keep what away from you, for God's sake?"

"The *bitchanna* are after me, the bloody *bitchanna*."

"What do you mean the *bitchanna*?"

"Can't you see them," said Blast, pointing with his hand. There, and there. Get rid of them, Father. Use your power."

"I don't see a thing, Blast." The priest was wondering was this some kind of a nightmare within a nightmare.

"You must be blind if you cannot see them bloddy *bitchanna*," Blast cowered even more, tring to drag the priest between him and what he was imagining he could see.

"If anyone is blind, I think it's you. Blind drunk. Have you been on the tear, or what?"

"I had a couple," Blast half answered, still concentrating on the *bitchanna*.

"A couple too many. How many?"

"A dropeen of the hard stuff I got for the cold earlier on."

"A dropeen? It's in the rats you are, Blast. You're seeing things, these bitches or *bitchanna*, or whatever it is you call them. Wait unti I get my hands on whoever it was gave you that much to drink."

"Well, it was myself gave it to myself, if you get my meaning. I had a bottleen of poteen in the stack of turf."

"A bottleen of poteen, and you drank a dropeen out of it?" Gibbons imitated Blast's accent.

"Precisely, Father."

"Would there be any chance that it was a big bottle, and that you finished it all off?"

"The good does be going out of it once you take the cork out of a bottle."

"And there isn't much point in putting the cork back on," the priest said, sarcastically.

"You have it now. Precisely."

"Come in with me to the sitting room, and I'll give you something to get rid of the bitches." George Gibbons pushed open the door of his study.

"It's not the pledge that you have in mind to give me?" Blast asked anxiously.

"I don't like giving what won't be kept." He poured a glass of whiskey for Blast, and another for himself. It was cold, and there was a bad taste in his mouth. "I want you to promise me that you will never drink poteen again. And if you do, I'm going to bring down a terrible curse on you, Blast."

"What kind of curse do you mean, Father?" Whatever if was could hardly be worse than the *bitchanna*.

"I'll tell Biddy about you being in the rats from drink." The priest handed Blast the whiskey, which he downed with a gulp. "Go home now, and sleep it off, like a good man."

"Everyone is down on me, Father," Blast said, a hangdog look in his eyes. "What makes you think that?"

"Biddy doesn't want me to be out after dark, and you're after giving me the pledge for the poteen. Sure soon there will be no pleasure at all left in life."

"Biddy is for your good, the same as I am. And if you have any sense you'll avoid getting into the rats again. I know now why you were seeing things the other night, the night the Anvy was supposed to have brought you home."

"She told on me."

"Everyone in the island knows about it. Sure, I heard you were boasting about it yourself. There are far too many people seeing things around here, far too much drinking going on."

Blast looked from his own empty glass to the priest's. "It was yourself that gave it to me, Father."

"Well, has it cured the *bitchanna*?"

"Do you know, but it has, thanks be to God," Blast said, heading for the front door. "I'll have to remember that one."

"You're a lost cause ..." George Gibbons laughed to himself, filling a nightcap to take upstairs. On second thoughts he thought it better to bring up the bottle. It was often difficult to get back to interrupted sleep.

Ω Ω Ω

Maggie had had a very difficult night with her mother, as often happened on the occasional night Sarah was unable to visit. Old Kate had shouted, complained, beat her stick on the floor for attention. Maggie had brought her water to drink, led her out on a fruitless mission to the toilet, given her a hotwater bottle, remained patient, kept her temper. At last the old woman had fallen into a fitful sleep. Downstairs Maggie kept the sound of the television very low so as not to disturb her. Then, all of a sudden, the shouting, the insults, the curses, the banging of the blackthorn on the floor started again. Maggie turned up the sound, hoping her mother would tire herself out and fall asleep.

There was such a loud bang then that she thought the old woman had fallen out of the bed. Maggie raced upstairs, only to find that it was not her mother that had fallen. She had knocked over a small bedside dressing table.

"What happened?" Maggie asked

"I had to knock it to attract your attention, that dirty thing down there along with you. I can hear the talk and the smooching."

"You can hear the television, mother." Maggie tried to straighten up the dressing table. "Look," she said, you have cracked the mirror." Her mother let out a screech of wild laughter. "Seven years of bad luck on you, you dirty little whore. Seven years bad luck on yourself and the hairyfella."

"I couldn't have any worse luck than to have to put up with you," Maggie snapped back at her, as she tried to remove the mirror, to prevent it splintering all over the floor. "How many mirrors did it take to bring that on me?"

"Ah, *marbhfháisc ort*," Kate used one of the old Irish curses that had lived on in the English language, the *marbhfháisc* being the strip of cloth tied around the head of a corpse to keep the mouth closed. Maggie lost her temper: "*Marbhfháisc* on yourself, and seven *marbhfháiscs*, and seven years and seven mirrors' bad luck on you, you ungrateful old bitch. That might shut your mean old mouth for you." The old woman raised her stick in the air, as if trying to hit her daughter, but it suddenly fell from her hand, as she began to cough and splutter, as if trying to vomit.

"What is it, mother? What's wrong?" Maggie's anger dissapated in a moment, quickly turning to concern. She noticed blood in the dribble from her mother's mouth. "Of all the nights I had to be on my own," she said. "I better send word for the priest, and the nurse." She cleaned Kate's mouth, and propped her up in the bed with pillows. The strength seemed to have just gone from her. Maggie hadn't time to check her pulse. She hurried downstairs, and ran through the night to call Sarah and Tomás. She hammered on their door and was still breathless when Tomás opened it. She told what had happened as best she could.

"Get the priest, Tomás," Sarah said, "and get him to ring the nurse. Go back to her Maggie. I'll be up to you as soon as I get Teresa to mind the kids." In her own mind she cursed Tomás's fear of the expense that had prevented them getting the phone into either house. Maggie headed home apprehensively, sensing that death would be there before her.

Father George Gibbons couldn't believe his ears when there was a knocking on his front door for the third time in one night. After his earlier experience he had left the light on over the stair-well, so he was able to open the door quickly to Tomás.

"Hurry, Father. I think the old woman is on her last."

"Which old woman?" asked the priest, slightly disorientated.

"Our old woman, Sarah's mother."

"Oh, old Kate ..." He hurriedly pulled on his soutane over his pyjamas, and was tying his shoes when Tomás asked "Will I wait for you?"

"No, carry on. I'll be fine." He was slightly amused with the old custom that the priest be accompanied on a sick call, in case the devil would accost him to prevent the salvation of a soul. That was one he would have to tell his priest friends.

"Would you mind if I rang the nurse from here?" Tomas asked hesitantly.

"Not at all. Just pull out the door after you when you are finished. I have to collect the oils and Communion from the sacristy." The priest hurried out the open front door, took the tabernacle from the safe in the sacristy, turned the lights on over the altar, and went to get the Holy Communion. With the corner of his eye he thought he saw somebody sitting very uprightly in a seat about half way down the church. He blinked, to clear the sleep from his eyes, and looked again. There was no one there, but he had taken with him an image of a hairy grey-bearded man. "It mustn't be only Blast that's seeing things," he told himself. He put on all the lights and walked the length of the chapel. There was nobody there, but the back door was open, gently swinging in the wind.

While he never locked the church, the priest always closed the door, to keep out wandering asses. He tried to remember had he closed it the previous night. Perhaps he had forgotten, he thought, when Daneen came to visit. He remembered the urgency of the call, and hurried to get the oils and communion, but the image of the grey-bearded man stayed with him.

Kate was dead when he reached the house. He anointed her, gave her the apostolic blessing, read the prayers for a happy death, prayers of consolation for the relatives, and said a decade of the rosary. Rising from his knees, George Gibbons sympathised with Maggie, and with Sarah, accepting the offer of a cup of tea. The body would be left a little while before the laying out would begin. There would be more prayers after that. As always the priest was surprised at how quickly people adjusted to the practicalities of death. There would be plenty of time for grief later on. Neighbours gathered in, offering prayers, sympathy and help.

"As nice a woman as I ever met, Maggie." Father Gibbons accepted the cup of tea and slice of buttered currant bread. "A saint, if ever there was one." For an awful moment he had an almost uncontrollable urge to laugh, remembering a monsignor from the diocese, who was wont to comment, on the death of over-reverent colleagues, "A saint, and like all saints, a bit of a shite."

"Sure the poor woman got no age at all." Blast, looking remarkably better than when the priest had seen him a few hours earlier, had entered with Biddy. Old Kate's death had been a lifesaver to him. He had come across the commotion connected with her sudden turn for the worse on his way home from the priest's house, and had managed to convey to Biddy that it was the emergency connected with the old woman's sudden illness that had kept him out so late. He hoped now that the priest would not inadvertently let the cat out of the bag on him.

"The woman could have another forty years in her," remarked Tomeen Rua, "only for the strokes she got."

"That's life."

"It's a day we all have to face."

"The will of God."

"We don't know the day nor the hour." All the usual words of consolation and resignation were rolled out. It didn't really matter who said them. It was the traditional way to get through the night of a death. The nurse had come and, with some local women who always took part in that ritual, helped Sarah and Maggie lay out the body.

"And they say she never smoked." In the kitchen George Gibbons added his bit to the conversation.

"Or drank either." Blast was always in his element on such occasions. Storytellers, characters were always necessary when there was a long night to be talked through. "It's many the one drank and smoked and got a longer life than the poor woman."

"Looking at it like that could drive a man to drink," Tomeen joked.

"She gave no battle at all, the poor woman." Bartley Mór thought that it was a little too early in the night to be making fun.

"The poor woman's time was up," Biddy commented.

There was silence for a time, each in their own thoughts on death, on life. George Gibbons, remembering again his experience from the chapel, thought that it would make a good conversation piece. He told the assembled people what happened. They seemed to take it a lot more seriously than he did himself.

"I don't think your eye would have taken such a clear picture of who was in it, if there was nobody there," Blast said.

"Sure I was only half awake. Daydreaming I was, or something"

"You must have got an awful fright," Biddy said.

"I got a far worse fright years ago on a sick call, when I heard the chains rattling." That got everyone's full attention. Blast blessed himself:

"God between us and all harm."

"I was called out from the college one night the priests of the parish were away at a meeting. When I had anointed the old man, his son offered to walk back with me. 'Not at all,' I said, 'sure I'm no length from the chapel,' and I wasn't either. What did I hear as I approached the church but a chain rattling inside the wall. I decided to muster up my courage and face the evil one. The sweat was coming out through me and I asked Jesus in the Holy Communion to protect me. I looked over the wall, where there was a field rising up in a little hill. On top of the hill between myself and the moon was the strangest sight I ever saw. It looked like a small little man with a short body and long legs. It had a big head and what looked like two big horns sticking up from the top of it. I was sure it was Satan himself until it began to bray and turned to one side at the same time. Was I pleased to hear that asses' roar and hear him dragging the chain he was tethered with along behind him. It goes to show how deceptive appearances can be."

"As long as you had your stole with you," Blast said, "you were alright. The stole," he explained to the gathering who knew it as well as himself, "is that long cloth a priest wears like a little scarf around his neck." He turned to the priest. "As long as you had your stole on you, you were as sound as a bell."

"Why do you say that?" Bartley asked. "Because that's where the power of the priest lies."

"You're not serious?" Tomeen said. "Would I be joking about the sacred mysteries of the church?"

"It wouldn't at all surprise me."

"Did you ever hear of the priest who lost his life because he let go of his stole?"

"Lost his life?" Daneen Shéamais, who had never intended speaking to Blast again, could not contain his curiosity.

"A man from a place called Carraroe told me this in the hospital. The same priest that was killed is buried within in the church there, he said. He was called out on a sick call a long way from home on a dark night. He did what he had to do, as our own good man did tonight, God bless him." Blast gave a little bow in the direction of George Gibbons. "On the way home across the fields, didn't a redhaired woman catch up to the priest. 'You seem to be worn out walking,' she said. 'I'll carry your coat for you a biteen of the way.' He gave her the coat, never thinking that he had left the stole in his pocket. What did she do, but kill him on the spot!"

"How?" Bartley asked the question on everyone's lips.

"She was a *sióg*."

"But how did she actually kill him?" Tomeen wanted to know.

"How does the wind blow? How does a bird fly?" Blast asked exasperatedly. "How do you expect me to know the workings of a *sióg*? They have their ways and means of doing things. Amn't I right, Father?" He looked to the priest for approval.

"That story is told, but as far as I know it's in the famine times it's supposed to have happened. The poor man might just have died of the hunger."

"How did they know it was a *sióg* if he was dead when they found him?" Daneen asked the logical questions. "And if it was dark how did they know she had red hair?"

Blast gave him a withering look. "Some people have no religion at all," he said.

"I'll have to keep a tight grip on my stole any more." The priest thought it time to intervene to prevent a row.

"At least the *sióg* in the church didn't kill you anyway," Tomeen said.

"There are those that say that drink is the cause of people seeing things." Blast had the priest where he wanted him. "But of course that wouldn't be the reason in your own case, as you're always pointing out the dangers that be involved in it."

"What I saw was nothing like a rat, anyway Blast." Gibbons hit back. "I doubt if I was in the rats from the drink." Daneen had another theory:

"I often heard it said, Father, that if a priest died without saying all the Masses he had promised, he would have to come back again and again until they were said. Maybe it was another priest you saw."

"If it was, Dan, then it was a hairy one." The priest was regretting ever having raised the subject. He would never live it down, and the result would probably be even more and worse superstition. He decided to try and limit the damage as best he could. "Anything is possible, I suppose. As Blast here has reminded me, maybe I had a bit too much of a nightcap and was a bit confused. That was all that was in it. Would ye mind now if I was to go? But we'll say a decade first for poor Kate." He pulled out his rosary beads. "What could we contemplate on more appropriate than the first glorious mystery of the most holy rosary, the resurrection of Our Lord Jesus Christ ..." Everyone shuffled down on to their knees.

They paused momentarily half way through the decade when a loud plaintive cry was heard somewhere in the distance. One or two people blessed themselves.

"The old dog must be missing her," Blast said, "the poor old bitch." The priest resumed the prayers, wondering was it the woman or the dog Blast was referring to.

The prayers over, the priest gone, the men went to the pub to get Edward Jack to set up a half barrel of porter in the house for the wake. They also bought whiskey, sherry, cigarettes and snuff. At the same time the women were giving the house a thorough cleaning, not that Maggie would have left a speck of dust anywhere, but because it was the traditional thing to do on such an occasion.

Ω   Ω   Ω

The Anvy had got a terrible shock when the lights had come on suddenly around the altar in the church. It was as if God was in some way answering his question, 'Do you know me? Do you recognise me?' He had sat as if stunned as the priest rushed on to the altar. For a split second he thought he might have been seen, but he had ducked quickly beneath the level of the top of the seats, crawled quickly down the side-aisle and let himself out the back door. Rather than running away he had waited in the shadows, knowing that it was only a sick call would have the priest out at that time of night.

It was clear almost immediately where the sick person was. One house stood out in a blaze of light, every window lit up. He had sensed it for a while. Kate. Aware of the need to be careful after a few recent experiences, the Anvy had hidden inside a high wall quite near Kate's house, watching people come from many directions. He feared the worst, but didn't venture near the house until all had gone quiet, nobody approaching the house any more. Crouching, with a piece of loose plastic hanging from his shoulder, he crept slowly towards the house until he could see in the window. People were getting on their knees to pray. She was gone. The Anvy ran blindly from the yard, releasing a screech of despair and sadness when he thought that he was out of earshot of the people at the wake. He ran and ran until he could be free, be himself, running across the wide sandy expanses of Trá Mhór.

Ω Ω Ω

Again and again the conversation at the wake came back to the figure the priest had seen, or thought he had seen, or pretended that he hadn't seen seen in the church earlier in the night. For many of the older people this world and the next faded in and out of each other, and their wonder had more to do with the excitement of something different than with fear of the unknown.

"Every one of the saints had a beard," Blast said with great conviction. "I wonder which one of them it was?"

"Are you gone completely out of your mind?" Biddy was the only person that would dare contradict him at that stage of the early morning, as he tended to get more agressive the more that he drank. "Are you trying to tell us that there are no women saints?"

"Pardon me, madam," Blast spoke as precisely as he could, "but I never said anything of the kind. Wasn't our own Saint Bridget a woman saint? Not to speak of Our Blessed Mother, the greatest saint of them all."

"Aren't you after telling us that every one of the saints had a beard? Are you saying that the women had beards as well?"

"Well, if it goes to that ..." Biddy interrupted him, fearing what most of the people present would consider an outrageous blasphemy. "Don't forget that we're in the house of the dead," she said, adding for effect, "The Lord have mercy on poor Kate."

"Amen," everyone replied in unision. The crisis had passed, as far as Biddy was concerned. The weather and the price of cattle were discussed in great detail, as well as the possibility of having an airstrip with daily landings as the islands of Aran had. It was Daneen that redirected their thoughts to the things of the other world.

"Maybe it was the light that made him disappear," he interjected out of the blue, as Bartley Mór was holding out on the benefits of sprouting potatoes before you set them. He had seen it done on a popular television soap opera and had tried it the previous year, having his first new potato on St. John's Eve, or bonfire night as it was known locally, almost a month earlier than the traditional St. MacDara's day.

"...Or maybe he was still there," Daneen continued, as his audience tried to come to terms with the sudden change of subject as they came to the end of a long, but not unpleasant night's wake. "He might have been there but Father George couldn't see him when he put the light on." Blast was impressed, his regard for Daneen's intelligence increasing by leaps and bounds. He blew a great burst of tobacco smoke from his mouth suddenly, letting it stand in the air before him. "Have a good look at that smoke," he said. "Correct me if I'm wrong, but a ghost is like that plume of smoke. You can see it and see through it at the same time."

"Now you're talking Blast ..." Bartley Mór was greatly taken by the explanation. "Didn't the priest say that the man he saw was pure grey all over. That's it, a man of smoke, a ghost. You're a genius, Blast."

"Did I say a ghost was a man of smoke?" Blast looked from face to face to see if anyone would dare contradict. "Did I say that?" He raised a finger, as a magician might do, to draw every eye. "I didn't say that at all, but I said you could see through a ghost the same way as you would look through smoke. It's not the same thing at all. He was probably still there but the priest couldn't see him. He could see through him instead. Has anyone a better idea than that?" He looked from eye to eye around the room.

Tomeen Rua decided to change the subject, to prevent Blast from getting too agitated.

"Wasn't there many a strange thing heard and seen in the past at times of death? Even the dog crying there when we were saying the rosary."

"That wasn't our dog," Maggie said quietly. "He's in Sarah and Tomás's so that he wouldn't be under people's feet here during the wake."

"Anyway, if there was to be something or somebody seen," Daneen said, "it's near the house you would expect it, not in the chapel." Tomeen shook his head, and spoke with great deliberation. "I've often heard of people seeing strange visons beyond in America, when some one belonging to them died here at home on the island."

Bartley came to his support "Didn't my own sister see my mother floating in a currach in a dream she had the night the mother died in the hospital." Accounts of one vision followed another as morning approached. But it was Maggie who really set people wondering when she said, "I think my mother did see the same vision around the house the priest saw in the church. Of course we didn't take a bit of heed of her. At least I didn't, I just thought that she was doting."

"God in heaven protect us!" Blast took off his cap and blessed himself. Sarah came to her sister's defence "You know the way it is with an old person. She used to imagine a lot of things. She was never right since she had that stroke."

"Sure she became an old woman overnight," Tomeen Rua said sympathetically.

"A fine cut of a woman she was in her day," Blast said with remembered admiration. "Goodlooking, airy, flighty as a young filly. No wonder she turned the head of the Yank."

Daneen gave a kind of a cough. Blast's comment were coming a bit too close to home as far as he was concerned. It was Biddy who redirected the conversation:

"If Kate was that fine of a woman, why didn't you go after her yourself?" Blast was seldom stuck for an answer. "The finest looking single woman I had in mind of course. Sure I had the finest woman of them all married to myself at the time."

"Whatever else you have lost, you haven't lost the *plámás*," Biddy said.

Daneen was still thinking of the priest's vision, as they were calling it at that stage. "Jesus himself," he said, bowing his head with respect,

"Our Lord himself had a beard, hadn't he? Maybe it was him Father George saw."

"But he wasn't grey," Blast reminded him. "He died a young man, the Lord have mercy on his soul."

"Maybe he got grey since," Biddy let out a screech of laughter, the sherry beginning to go to her head. "I wouldn't be a bit surprised, with all that he has to put up with."

Ω Ω Ω

Teresa Shéamaisín was minding Sibéal and Patricia for Sarah and Tomás while they were at the wake and the funeral. She had been at home with her father since completing her Leaving Certificate a year and a half earlier. Living on the dole and with her father's pension to help, they got by, but she always appreciated the extra few pound that was to be earned from babysitting and childminding. She hoped to get on a Government work-experience or training course, but she had heard nothing from the Employment Exchange about it for a long time. She had been glad of the break from school, particularly as she had to go to a boarding school on the mainland, as their was no secondary education provided on the island.

Although she tried hard to read or concentrate on television when the children were asleep, Teresa could only think of one thing, Edward Jack and the terrible thing he had said to her. "The best ride on the island." She wouldn't mind if she had been with anyone other than himself. That hurt her far more than the messing that went on beside the hall the night of the disco. He was a right bastard, she told herself, but she couldn't get him out of her mind. Maybe she was in love with him? she asked herself, replying vehemently, "I hate the fucker."

To give the children a sense of security while their father and mother were at the wake, Teresa had slept with them in their parent's bed. She awoke in the early morning to find that she had her period, the sheets in a mess. She had been so sure that she was not going to get it that she had made no preparation, taken no precaution. She hoped to have the sheets washed and dried before Sarah was finished with the funeral. It wasn't that she would not understand, but Teresa felt ashamed. At least she had managed to hide it from the children, tickling and cuddling them before they got up, giving them the task of setting the table for breakfast, while she surreptitiously changed the sheets.

Now that the period had arrived, she almost regretted not being pregnant. Now that she thought properly about it, she probably wasn't past her time at all. Because she was so regular she hardly bothered with dates. Thinking back over the previous month, it was very likely that she had made four weeks out of three, because of her worry, her certainty that she was pregnant.

She had been sure of what she would do. She would rear her child herself on the island. There would be a single mother's allowance, and having their own potatoes and vegetables as well as her father's pension, they would be comfortable enough. Much easier than trying to raise a child on your own in a city flat. She would avoid men like the plague, she had told herself. Her father would provide a father figure for his grandchild. If he was good with her – she thought it would be a girl – as he had been with herself, the child would lack nothing in love and affection.

Teresa loved children and really enjoyed caring for Sibéal and Patricia. About midday she took them to their grandmother's house, to see her laid out in the locally made white wooden coffin. Sarah and Tomás had thought long and hard about this, Tomás thinking the children should be spared the pain of it, Sarah thinking that it was important that they understand the realities of life and death. "After all death is the most inevitible thing in life," she had argued. "It's part of human nature, especially when someone has reached a decent age." They had come to a kind of compromise. The children would be brought to the house, but not to the cemetry until the grave was closed. Tomás had remembered the stones thudding on his grandfather's coffin when he was a small boy, and had many nightmares subsequently.

Sibéal was full of questions after visiting the wakehouse. "Why is Mammo so cold? Where is she now? Have they television in Heaven? Would she see Jesus? Why did he always have that apple-thing in his hand?" referring to the Sacred Heart picture. Before leaving her grandmother's she had told Sarah matter-of- factly that she wanted Teresa as her mother when she died herself. Sarah, while having a good laugh at the child's innocence, wondered had the reality of death come across too strongly, or was the child just recognising that everyone died?

The children had gone to sleep, or at least to bed, and Teresa was ironing the sheets she had washed that morning when there was a knock at the door. Teresa tried to close the door in his face when she saw that it was Edward. "You're not welcome here," she said. But he had his foot on the threshold preventing the door closing.

"I didn't realise that it was your house," he said with a smile. "When did you buy it? The previous owners said that I was welcome at any time."

"Tomás and Sarah are not here as you well know. There are up at the corpse-house if you want to see them."

"I saw them. I'm just after coming from there." Edward gave the impression that they knew he was calling to their house. Teresa relented, and let him inside. "I wanted to talk to you," he said.

"We have absolutely nothing to talk about."

"I came to say I'm sorry."

"Sorry was never in time," Teresa repeated the old saying. "What good is sorry now?"

"I've thought a lot about us since." Edward sat beside the range. Teresa stood with her back to the dresser, the kitchen table between them.

"About us?" She folded her arms, intent on making him squirm, delighted in her heart of hearts that he had called, apologised.

"I was thinking ..." He was a great man for the witty remarks in the pub or shop, but found himself at a loss for words to express himself now. "I thought that maybe it wouldn't be the worst thing that could happen, you and me, like."

"What, in the name of God are you trying to say, Edward?"

"Why don't the two of us get married?" he blurted out. Despite herself, Teresa laughed.

"God, but you're the romantic one, Edward Jack. I've heard it all now." Imitating him, "Why don't the two of us get married? What a proposal..."

"What am I supposed to say? This isn't easy for me, you know."

"Have you been drinking?"

"I had one pint at the wake."

"Well, it's gone to your head."

"I'm serious about this." Edward nodded his head a couple of times to emphasise how serious he was.

"Well, I'm touched," Teresa said with a little sarcasm. "You are going to accept your responsibilities, to marry the best ride on the island, who you happened to put up the pole."

"I didn't mean that." Edward cringed. "I was just so shocked, so mad. I know you don't fuck around."

"No, I'm not a man, up on every middle-aged bimbo that needs a gigilo during the summer holidays." Teresa thought it great to get an opportunity to say all the things she had rehearsed in her mind all week. "Anyway it's not right to marry because a baby is on the way." She felt she was in a strong position, now that she had her period.

"Who said that?"

"Father George."

"You've told him." Edward was astonished. "He admitted parentage, or parenthood, or whatever you call it." Teresa kept a straight face, despite the outrageousness of her statement, knowing the priest in question. "The priest?"

"Isn't that why they call him Father George." Teresa felt lightheaded, and laughed uproariously.

"Have you been drinking?" Edward turned her earlier question back on her.

"Only the wine of love and romance." She acted as if she was waltzing with herself around the kitchen.

"What did Gibbons say, really?" Indifferent about religion himself, Edward was all too aware what it meant to his parents, and how close they were to the priest.

"I was just quoting what he said one Sunday recently, the day he wasn't talking about drink. Of course his voice might not have been strong enough to reach out to the yard." Teresa was really enjoying herself at Edward's discomfiture.

"Well, how about it anyway?"

"Is that a proposal?"

"You could call it that. Look it, it's not the child, but until then I hadn't thought seriously about marriage. It made me think what the hell? Why not? You could do worse."

"What a compliment to a woman – you could do worse."

"You're the finest, really"

"As well as being the best ride on the island?" Edward knew from the way she smiled that the ice had been broken, so he risked a joke. "I'm inclined to exaggerate, sometimes."

Teresa went over towards him, and jokingly made as if to hit him. They were in each other's arms in seconds, kissing passionately. When thay paused for breath, Teresa asked:

"It is only because of the child, isn't it?"

"It is mine, as well, isn't it? I shouldn't say that," he corrected himself. "It's ours, though I still don't know how it happened."

"Did they teach you anything at all in that fancy college?" Teresa asked.

"Like what?"

"Like the facts of life, how babies are made? Well, that's how it happened, except that it didn't happen."

"You were fooling me all along?" Teresa told him of the previous night.

"You might not believe me. I have just destroyed the evidence," she said. "That's why I'm ironing the sheets."

"Thank God for that," Edward said, relieved. "You knew all along, and let me make an *amadán* of myself?"

"By asking me to marry you? That's making an *amadán* of yourself, is it?"

"No. I still want to marry you, but I'm glad that it is not to be done under pressure." He kissed her on the lips. "Well, what have you to say?"

"Thank you."

"Thank you, you will or you won't marry me?"

"Thank you, I don't know."

"You don't know what?"

"I don't know if we know each other well enough."

"What can we learn that we don't know now?"

"We learnt ..." Teresa corrected herself. "I learned an awful lot in the past couple of weeks."

"I did too, but that's over now."

"I'll give you your answer at Christmas," she said.

"Sounds reasonable enough."

"In the meantime, none of that carry on." She removed the hand that was carressing her through her jeans.

"We're nearly engaged. We're entitled to the old coort."

"Kissing and cuddling are fine ..."

"I suppose I'll have to make do," Edward joked, "with the best kisser and cuddler in the island."

"And I'll be keeping a close eye on you when those old biddies of bank clerks and teachers come around here in the summer, looking for their oats."

"They will have to make do with the juice of the barley instead. I wouldn't mind but I never laid a hand on one of the old bitches."

"You could see them melting every time you looked at them."

"Wasn't it you that was keeping a close eye on me?"

"Blast's Biddy was right. You are a handsome old hunk, or should I put it in your own words, you're not the worst."

"There wouldn't be any old dropeen in the press? We could have a bit of a celebration."

"For what?"

"We did make up, didn't we? Even if we got no farther."

"I don't own the place," Teresa said primly. "You know where they keep it?"

"That's another thing that can't be overdone between now and Christmas," Teresa laid down the law, "the drink."

"What time of the night will we be getting up to say the prayers?" Edward asked, tongue in cheek.

"What prayers?"

"Now that you have decided to make a monk out of me, you're as well to go all the way," he joked. "You'll soon have me as much under control as Biddy has Blast, and us not married at all."

"The day anyone manages to get you under control, that will be the day."

"Sure you have me wound around your little finger already."

"You'll have to bring me to see Mammy and Daddy one of these days," Teresa joked.

"I wouldn't rush it if I were you."

"I know well that I won't be good enough for their pet."

"It's not that, but my father seems to have got the impression that you are pregnant, and pressurising me into marriage."

"What would make him think that?"

"He claims that everyone has it."

"Well it might come as a bit of a surprise to them when nine months go by. Though knowing the minds of some of them around here, I'll probably be accused of having an abortion."

"Does it matter what anyone thinks, so long as we're together?"

"That was a lovely thing to say, Edward. Who knows, you might even tell me one of these days that you love me?"

"Doesn't every kiss say that?" They were kissing, Teresa sitting on Edward's knees when Sarah pushed in the back door. "Excuse me," she said, a smile from ear to ear on her face, remembering how recently Teresa had told her that she detested Edward. "And me thinking that poor Teresa would be lonely after the children went to bed."

"How are things up at the house?" Edward asked.

"It's mainly the family there tonight," Sarah replied, "since the lads got home, and we took her to the church. I think everyone is trying to get a night's sleep before the funeral." She went to the hot press to get the clothes she had come back for. "Did the children go down alright for you?"

"She bate enough out of them." Edward was back to his old repartee. "They sleep great after the tears."

"They were grand. I was just going to tuck them in." Sarah went quickly to the room and hugged the sleeping children. "Well," she said, when she came back to the kitchen, "I won't be disturbing you."

"I'm off myself as well," Edward arose, gently sliding Teresa from his lap.

"Don't go because of me," Sarah said.

"Tomorrow will be a busy day." He felt embarrassed when he had said it, as if they would be making money in the pub from the other's grief. "Goodnight."

"You're doing alright there." Sarah winked at Teresa, as Edward went out the door.

"What a difference a day makes ..."

$$\Omega \ \Omega \ \Omega$$

Unknown to the world the Anvy was at Kate's funeral. He hid in the clumps of ivy growing on the rocks across from the church while

Mass was in progress. He heard the voice of the priest coming out on the loudspeakers as he talked of how nice and how kind Kate was. There was no talk of her flightiness, of her letting down the man she was to marry. But what would the priest know about that? the Anvy thought. He could smell the incense as the coffin was carried from the church.

He waited until the cortege had moved away towards the cemetry, and then crossed wall after wall, as he went from field to field until he reached the lower road. He knew that anyone in the place that was capable of walking would be at the funeral. But it was as well to be careful and avoid the danger of being detected.

The Anvy had long experience of running in a stooped gait, so that he would not be seen over the height of a wall. In so far as that was possible he had perfected a kind of camouflage, carrying a bit of torn plastic hanging from his head and shoulders, giving the impression to anyone who saw it that it was a piece of sacking blowing in the breeze. So many things, from hay to sea-rods were protected from rain by pieces of plastic that is was a very convenient camouflage.

He circled around the goatpath at the back of the graveyard and was in the next field, stooped in a fissure between the rocks long before the funeral arrived. They were delayed as the coffin was passed from each group of six men to the next as they took turns to carry the coffin the mile and a half to the graveyard. The Anvy tightened the plastic about him on hearing the murmer of conversation as the people arrived at the graveside, near the shore, not thirty yards from where he crouched.

He heard the monotone of the priest intone the prayers, and different people take turns in leading the five decades of the rosary. At the same time he could hear the stones and soil thud on Kate's coffin. The prayers ceased. From days gone by the Anvy knew that each family would scatter around the cemetery to say prayers at the graves of their own dead. It was better not to move for some time.

When he heard the heavy steps come in his own direction a little while later, he knew that it was his brother, Daneen. He held himself motionless, like a rabbit, as silent as the dead. Daneen obviously took no notice of what was beneath the plastic in the *scailp*. The Anvy felt the warmth of his brother's piss as it splashed all over the thin covering. He heard Daneen limp away, but remained in the same crouched, painful position until he felt sure that literally the coast was clear.

Ω Ω Ω

Maggie was on her own at last. The funeral was over, her brothers gone back to England. As one of them had said, "Work is so scarce that if you're more than a couple of days away, there is someone else in your place." Everyone seemed to be worried about her, but all Maggie herself felt was relief. She had peace and quiet at last. As the priest had intoned the words 'eternal rest' again and again from the church ritual, Maggie felt that she needed that rest more than her mother did.

Would her contentment soon turn to loneliness? she wondered. At that stage she could not care. The constant calling, cursing, insults were all over. The cleaning, wiping, washing from morning until night. Peace at last.

Sarah had not been to visit as much. She was tired too after the wake and the funeral. She needed to spend time with the children. Anyway Maggie could visit them now as often as she wanted. She was not housebound any more, a prisoner of her mother's demands.

Now that she was free to go wherever she wanted, Maggie did not want to go anywhere. She didn't care if she was never to see the mainland. Let the world come to her, she felt, through the television set in the corner. Later on it would be nice maybe to go to the city with Sarah, look at the clothes in the shop windows, maybe buy something, even. Right now all she wanted was time to herself.

She had told the story of her mother's death so often that she felt she had a longplaying record in her head, the selfsame story for everyone that came to the wake. She had told nobody, not even Sarah, what the last words that passed between herself and her mother were.

"*Marbhfháisc...*" The curse had worked, she told herself with a wry smile. At that moment it didn't bother her one bit. She had peace, quiet, contentment, at last.

She knew that people thought she would be afraid in the house on her own, afraid of her mother's ghost, or something. There had been all kinds of offers, of people who would sleep in at night, that sort of thing. Maggie didn't care in the slightest about what she might see or not see. She had put up with worse than any ghost for years. What could she see that would be less hateful, poisonous, insulting than her mother had been?

It was not that she hated her mother. She just did not feel anything for her, except maybe a little pity. Pity because of what her strokes had done to her, how they had changed her. Maggie had no doubt but she herself would take an overdose if she got the same illness. She could not place that burden on anyone, she felt.

What would she do with herself all day long she wondered? Knitting, maybe. It would pass the time, earn a few extra pounds. She would miss the pension coming into the house, but she would have her dole. What expenses would she have? She would live on what she could gather on the shore if she had to, she told herself. From a health point of view what could be better than that?

'Life begins at forty,' people used to say. Maggie was within a couple of years of that and could see a whole new life opening up before her. The doctors in the psychiatric hospital had told her she should, as thay put it "leave her environment," that her life with her mother on the island had contributed to her being hospitalised. She had not left her environment, she thought, so much as that her environment had now changed itself.

Her thoughts went back to the people she had met and got to know in the long high bare halls of that hospital, many of their lives destroyed, not by a hereditary illness but from the lot that befell them in life, family circumstances, family rows, a lousy hand dealt them in the game of life. Maggie knew now that she would never have to enter those big grey forbidding buildings again. It was as if she had passed through her purgatory and was about to enter some kind of heaven. Any heaven would do, so long as it was better than what she had gone through, she thought. She never felt better. She was alive, and wasn't it great to be alive?

Ω Ω Ω

There was no talk of the Anvy for a long time. People were busy with the spring work, drawing seaweed, making ridges, planting, sowing. It was as if the Anvy was forgotten as soon as the days began to lengthen. George Gibbons, the priest was amused by this, confirming a theory he had, or a comment someone had made, that the Anvy was a figment of the imagination used to help pass long winter nights. As the days got longer and warmer, he began to stir out more from his reading, to walk the roads, to breathe the fresh sea air, to chat with the people as they worked in the fields.

It pleased him to see the women out working side by side with the men in many cases. They were not doing the heavy work of old, carrying creels of seaweed from the tide, as their mothers and grandmothers had done. He had heard of women who had babies born on the shore, they had worked so far into pregnancy. Most of the women now just helped with the planting, as if the vegetable section of the field was something too difficult or complicated to leave to a man.

One beautiful evening he walked out as far as the Caladh Beag, a small inlet from which currachs were launched in the summer to fish for lobster. The priest sat for a long time looking at long, large, slow waves breaking themselves on the shore, hangovers from some big storm out in the great Atlantic. He sat on a rock, thinking it was a great life to be able to while away a day in such a fashion. But his mind was not used to idleness. He pulled a notebook from his pocket after a time, and began to write a sermon. There was something in the clear air that awakened thoughts, that stirred imagination.

He wrote of the beauty of the world, the damage done by pollution. To bring the matter nearer home he wrote of the rubbish being dumped indiscriminately here and there on the island, of little plastic rings that were made to hold beer-cans which choked seabirds. Pollution was not just something that happened far away at nuclear generating stations. It happened everywhere, even on their own couple of square miles, God's work of creation being spoiled by neglect and carelessness. He was about to continue, to write of how people's lives were polluted by the abuse of alcohol. Someone had given him a strong hint that he had beaten the subject of drink to death, so he decided to give it a rest, at least until after Easter.

The priest made his way west along the coast, a difficult place in which to walk among the rocks thrown ashore by the sea, but a beautiful place, the scenery improving as Trá na gCapall was approached from the Northern direction. As he walked, he had to watch where he stepped, as it would be very easy to break an ankle among the rocks. It surprised him to hear the steel blade of a spade clanging on a stone quite near to where he walked. Who would be setting a crop so far from the houses?

George Gibbons made his way to the high stone wall and, stretching himself, looked in across it. Daneen Shéamais was working away, down on his knees, about which he had tied canvas bags for protection. He must have powerful arms, the priest thought to himself, as he watched Daneen, the handle of the spade held halfway, trench up the side of a ridge. Daneen looked happy, his earphones on his ears as he worked away.

Gibbons thought he would slip away without letting Daneen know he was ever there. His method of digging might be some kind of embarrassment to him, and anyway how could you say "God bless the work" to a man with earphones. But Daneen had spotted the movement at the top of the wall with the side of his eye. He straightened up, removing the earphones.

"Isn't it a lovely day, Father, thanks be to God."

"The best day this year, Dan, without a doubt." He went in the gap, asking God to bless the work at the same time. "And you can call it work," he said admiringly. "Sure you will never eat that many potatoes in a year?"

"Sure if I don't the hens will. And I was thinking of getting a pig. The meat would be healthier than what you would buy in a shop, with all the chemicals and everything the put in it nowadays."

"I'm delighted to see," the priest said, "people showing so much interest in the environment."

"From the radio I learned all about that kind of thing. You're doing a healthy thing yourself, Father, out walking in the fresh air."

"Not as healthy as what you're doing." He felt a sense of shame that he was out just passing the time, a lame old man like Daneen working hard in his field. "It's hard work that there with the loy." He tried to impress Daneen with his knowledge of farm instruments, remembering Synge's playboy who had killed his father with a blow from a loy.

"A spade we call it ourselves, Father, though they have the other word in some places."

"You must have a great pair of arms."

"It's a pity the legs are not as strong as them," Daneen said.

"Is it how you had an accident?" The priest felt familiar enough with him now to ask a personal question.

"It was the old TB, if you ever heard of it."

"I heard of little else when I was a young fellow," answered George Gibbons.

Daneen told him his own history, standing knee-deep in the water when they were building the seawall, the years in the sanatorium. "When I look at all that died from it," he concluded, "I suppose that I'm lucky to be alive. The will of God, I suppose, Father."

The priest looked on that approach as a kind of fatalism. "I doubt that God wanted so many people to suffer and die from TB, it's just that he was not going to interfere in that aspect of humanity." Thinking he was losing Daneen in this kind of surmising and sermonising, he decided to use a positive tack. "Let's say that it must have been the will of God that a cure was found for it, and the will there to tackle the problem. A lot of credit is due to Doctor Noel Browne, who was Minister for Health at the time."

"He wasn't a man that the clergy used to praise a lot, the same Doctor," Daneen made his point as diplomatically as he could.

"Sure the clergy can talk a lot of old *seafóid* too."

"You are only joking me now, Father." Daneen was not going to be drawn into criticising the clergy. "Where would we be at all without the priests and the Mass?"

"You would make a fine priest yourself, Dan, you have more faith than I have."

"But sure I never got the learning."

"Faith is more important than education in this job. If I was bishop myself, I would ordain you, and leave the island to you. That would soon solve the shortage of priests."

"I wouldn't be able for it." Daneen was shaking his head. "I wouldn't be able to face the kind of thing you faced in the church the other night."

"You mean the night old Kate died?" Gibbons had rarely thought of it since. "Sure the two of us talked so much of ghosts the same night, it was no wonder that I was seeing things."

"Nothing would frighten a priest," Daneen said admiringly, "God's messenger on earth."

"God's messenger or not, we're as human as the rest. It's not long since I heard a man say on a television programme that he believes in God at night, but that he doesn't during the day. Darkness can be very deceptive, make you think there is something there when there's not." Not for the first time George Gibbons found himself trying to rationalise what others accepted as part of nature, the natural and supernatural coexisting.

"In the old days a lot of people who had died used be seen walking the roads at night, or out fishing," Daneen said. "That was the time there was a lot of trawl-line fishing going on for bream."

"There was a lot of poteen drank at that time. It was not just the electricity that did away with the ghosts, but the missioners as well, preaching against the poteen."

"Some say there's no harm in poteen, if it's made properly."

"I suppose that might be true," the priest agreed, "but when it's cheap, people are inclined to drink too much of it."

"Some of the missioners were inclined to overdo it a bit, Father."

"They preached the gospel as best they could." Gibbons came to the defence of his fellow clergy, "in season and out of season."

"They frightened people a bit too much."

"When police and Government could not get rid of the curse of the poteen, what choice had they?"

"I remember the night the big missioner flung the crucifix down the aisle of the chapel," Daneen said with the clarity of a man describing something he could still see with the eyes of his mind. "A lot of people lost faith in him, Father, when he hadn't more respect than that for the cross of Christ."

"When you look at it like that, I suppose ..." Daneen didn't give him time to finish, as he went on to recount what happened the night the big missioner, as he was known on the island, threw the cross. "I was only a boy at the time, but I knew that everyone in that church was scared. They thought he had put a curse on the whole parish by firing the holy cross down among the people. Next day the stills and the barrels and the worms were gathered into a heap on that *creig* beyond the church. They still call it *creig a' phoitín*, because it was mainly the Irish that was used here among the old people at that time. It was said that it wasn't the best equipment that people had that went in the big bonfire, that the good stills were kept to make a drop for the following winter."

"Nothing like keeping your options opened," the priest joked. Daneen continued:

"I happened to be standing beside the missioner, looking up at him, a fine cut of a man he was. He sent me in to the priest's house to get a coal from the fire and bring it out on a shovel. I remember how the big missioner caught the handle of the shovel in one hand, as another person would take a spoon. He fired the burning coal in at the butt of the heap of barrels and stills and worms. Sure the whole lot was soaked in poteen and it went up in a big shot of flame, with black smoke rising from the top of it. "Did ye see Satan going up in the flames?" the big missioner roared. There was many a man there, and woman too that would swear to this day that they saw the devil rising from the poteen, but I didn't see him. Others said they saw a hare as big as a goat running away over the *creig*, even though there never were hares on this island, only plenty of rabbitts."

"Maybe it was the Anvy that ran out of the fire" the priest joked.

"Strangely enough," Daneen said, "there was no talk at all of the Anvy when I was a boy. It was years later that all that started."

"Well, at least," the priest commented, "the poteen was got rid of."

"There was never as much of it after that, though there used be a drop made for Christmas, or if there was a wedding, though there are very few of them nowadays."

"As tough as the big missioner was on the poteen," George Gibbons wanted to say something positive about his fellow priest, "he was supposed to be easy to go to confession to."

"That used to be said," Daneen agreed, "but people used to work the head on him as well."

"I can't imagine that was easy to do."

Daneen explained:

"People didn't want to have to tell him a lie in the confession box, so they would make sure they saw him arriving in the parish. When he asked them in confession - "Have you made or have you drank poteen since you saw me last?" thay were able to answer truthfully 'Not since I saw you last, Father,' having seen him the day before."

"Isn't it on the poor foolish priest you are able to work the head too," the priest joked.

"There's no need to any more, Father." Gibbons had a great laugh at Daneen's answer:

"We're such *amadáns* now that you don't need to work the head on us at all!"

"That's not what I mean, but priests nowadays are not as bad-tempered as they used to be long ago."

"Maybe that's what has left the religion the way it is," Gibbons replied.

"Sure the faith is a lot better now than it was in them times. There isn't as much fear involved in it."

"I'm glad to hear you say that, Dan. So many people talk of the good old days and the way things used to be. But I agree with you, there was far too much fear, and not enough of the love of God and the neighbour." Thinking about his tea, and trying to prevent Daneen getting another theological conversation going, the priest signed off: "I have wasted enough of your time, Dan."

"The day is long, Father, and the year is longer."

George Gibbons walked on. The shortest way home at this stage was up by Trá na gCapall. His thighs and calf muscles were beginning to pain him, jumping from rock to rock, stepping higher or lower on the rough terrain. But he felt great, his head clear, easy in his mind. What a difference to the many years he had spent teaching, cooped up in a stuffy room until four o' clock in the afternoon. "Years ago I should have got out of it," he told himself, as he breathed the clear air into his lungs in the method he had learnt many years before from the elocution master in the seminary.

Father Gibbons knew at the same time that it would have broken his heart if he had been sent to the island immediately after his ordination.

The notion of being placed on an island was something similar to going to purgatory among himself and his contemporaries. Too many had had nervous breakdowns on islands, partly because they did not know when their 'sentence' was going to end. It was a sentence for many as the islands tended to be used as punishment stations for priests who dirtied their copybooks in any way, particularly by indulging too much in alcohol, or writing articles for the press. 'Ink and drink' had been the curse of many a priest in the old days. Women had seemed a minor temptation by comparison.

As far as he was concerned the best thing that had ever happened in the diocese was the arranging of an equal basic pay for all the clergy. A man on an island of a couple of hundred people no longer lived in poverty, while his counterpart in a biggish town got a little extra because of the extra burden of work.

An out of the way parish with a beautiful golf course by the sea had become the heart's desire of many of his colleagues, altough described by the same men in the past as the 'arsehole' of the diocese.

When he was approaching Trá na gCapall from the northern end, Gibbons laughed to himself about the day the Mass servers had brought him there in search of the Anvy. The whole idea of something like that being present on a small island defied logic. It was like the Loch Ness monster or the abominable snowman, a myth wheeled out for amusement during the media's silly season, or in what the dramatist John Millington Synge used to describe as the long nights after Samhain.

The flash of a vision he thought he saw in the church had come back to haunt him time after time in the following days, though he had just forgotten about it after a while. What amazed him was that it had stood out so clearly in his mind. His father had lost his reason to a great extent due to hardening of the arteries in the years before his death. George Gibbons wondered could the same be beginning to happen to himself. He put the notion out of his mind with the mental direction to himself to "think positive." The evening was too fine for brooding.

As he stood at the top of the storm-beach, or *duirling*, at Trá na gCapall the priest noticed Bartley Mór down on the shoreline gathering sea-rods from the red seaweed thrown ashore by the high sea. He climbed down over the rounded stones to greet him.

"Are they plentiful this year, Bartley?"

"The best year I ever remember, Father, sure there has been a swell in the sea almost every week since Christmas. We had a lot of bad weather before the recent good spell."

"Do you think that it will stay settled?"

"You'll get about another ten days like this."

"Even the weather forecasters on the television and the radio are not as sure about it as that. It's a great skill to have," George Gibbons said admiringly.

"This last new moon came in standing up. She was on her back for most of the winter before that. You get a lot of storms when the moon is on her back."

"You'll make your fortune this year so, Bartley, plenty of sea-rods and the fine weather to harvest them."

"I think it is only in your job the fortunes are to be made, Father," Bartley joked. "It's the only job in which you can pass around a basket and collect your week's wages."

"I'd be a bit surer of myself collecting sea- rods."

"I'll swop with you anytime you like. These yokes," Bartley said, holding up one of the rods, "they reduce almost to nothing when they are drying. It takes a lot of gathering to get a ton of them."

"You would think the good would be gone out of them when they reduce so much."

"All that they lose is the water. As far as I know anyway. I haven't much skill in things like that. It's small the factory wants them, so it's small that they get them. They use them to make iodine or something. All I care about is the few pounds that they bring in to top up the dole, but don't be telling that to the guager."

"Isn't that what you call the person who checks up on people earning the dole? I hear he is worse to see coming than the Anvy."

"More often than not it's a she, and they are the worst of the lot."

"You would think that Government officials would have better to do than pursuing people on a little island for a miserable few pounds. It's the big bucks that get away with it, the politician's friends, as came out in recent years."

"It's a funny thing that there would be no government guager after me if I was to spend all day long on a high stool up in Black Jack's, but if I spend a while gathering the sea-rods that help to keep a factory going, I'm bad news."

"In fairness to the guager," George Gibbons always tried to see the good side in everyone, "I suppose he or she is only doing a job." Bartley didn't agree:

"The way some of them go about it you would think the likes of me was stealing out of their own pocket. They are too mean altogether about it."

"Well, I won't be informing on you anyway, Bartley." The priest began to climb back over the slippery stones. He paused for a moment as Bartley advised him to avoid the rocks that had a green kind of moss on them. As he stood, his eyes were drawn to the serrated edge of the clifftop overhanging Trá na gCapall, silhouetted now in the weak rays of a sinking Spring Sun. "Wouldn't the top of the cliff remind you of a castle," he said to Bartley.

"Now that you mention it," Bartley put his hand up to shield his eyes from the sun, "it's true for you." His eyes were sharper than the priests from years of watching out for wrack. "Who is that up on top of it?" he asked.

"Is there someone there?" The priest tried to focus his eyes against the sun.

"I saw a figure moving up there a minute ago. It was like a goat standing up on it's hind legs, but it seemed to drop down then in the *scailp*."

"I didn't see a thing with the sun in my eyes."

"Daneen Shéamais' old *pocaide* is often around there. A dangerous yoke he is if he was to go after you. I don't think he would have any more respect for a man of the cloth than for the next man. He gave an awful thump in the backside to one of the tourists that was wandering around there last summer."

"I'll watch out for him," the priest said. "I suppose you will soon be finishing up yourself. It would be an awkward place to get out of in the dark."

"I'll have a few more bundles gathered before dusk. There will be no guager likely to come around at this time of the day."

Ω Ω Ω

Teresa and Edward were enjoying their courtship even though they were well aware of the rumours that she was pregnant and was forcing him to marry her. There was only one way to prove the gossip mongers wrong, let them wait and wait for the baby that wasn't on the way.

They had walked every inch of the island during the fine nights of late spring while the moon grew and waned. There was little else to do. The discos had stopped until the secondary school children would be home from boarding school at Easter. Neither felt like staying in and watching television when they could be out together in the open air. As they walked the great sandy expanse of Trá Mhór Edward felt that the silence had gone on too long.

"Isn't it great weather, altogether?"

"Well isn't it really wonderful weather," Teresa said sarcastically. "The finest spring in years. And the forecast is good for another few days. Only for the same weather what would there be to talk about? Weather, weather, weather. My father talks of nothing else from morning until night, and now you are at it too."

"A fellow has to start someplace. You're not very talkative yourself."

"There is more to life than weather."

"Tell me about it so." Edward put an ear over near her mouth.

"Cut that out," Teresa said sharply. "Why should I have to do all the talking?"

"Because you are not satisfied with what I have to say."

"You have no shortage of smart talk in the bar and the shop. Pretend that I'm a customer. What do you talk to them about?"

"The weather."

"You're full of shit, Edward Jack."

"Surely people don't have to be talking non-stop all the time. I didn't walk all the way down to here to start fighting and arguing."

"Who is fighting and arguing?"

"You are, my love, my life, my joy," Edward said, with a theatrical flourish.

"Keep your old *seafóid* for your customers.

It's me you're talking to now."

"Well, where will I start? Politics?

Literature? Religion? Sex?"

"You're trying to make an óinseach out of me now."

"I can't win," Edward said in exasperation. "You're no óinseach, but two are needed to keep up a conversation."

"You have no shortage of things to say when there are young ones in the bar."

"I have to keep my customers in humour," he answered airily.

"You do that alright."

"Do I detect a little jealousy here?"

"O, Edward!" Teresa put her arms around him. "It drives me crazy the way thay go on about how handsome you are. You could have any woman you want."

"I know that," he said cockily, before hugging Teresa, "and I have."

"That's what I wanted to hear. You mean that?"

"Would I be here if I didn't?"

"You're not getting tired of me, are you?"

"We're not doing anything that would tire me out," he joked.

"That isn't everything."

"It's something."

"We can break up if you like."

"What kind of daft *seafóid* has got into you at all?" Edward shook her gently, as Teresa squeezed her arms about him.

"I just wanted to know if you still loved me."

"Of course I do." He kissed her. They hugged and kissed, tumbling in the sand. Edward loosened Teresa's bra, and pushing up her jumper, took her breast in his mouth. He was expecting every minute to be pushed away, but all Teresa did was joke:

"Your mammy mustn't have given you enough tit when you were small."

"She did, and plenty,' he raised his head. "A lot more than I get from you."

"Go home to mammy so," Teresa said, playfully, jumping up quickly and running along the sand, laughing, Edward in hot pursuit. Her speed amazed him, but he managed to bring her down with a rugby tackle.

"You have me nearly killed," she joked. "Now you can't say that I learned nothing at that fancy college, as you call it.'

"Rugby snobs," Teresa said, crawling away from him.

"I didn't ask to be sent there," he said, catching her right leg and hauling her back to him. They tickled and kissed and hugged and rolled around in the sand. Edward was trying to open the belt of Teresa's jeans when he sensed there was someone quite close, watching them. "Hey," he said, jumping up. The stooped figure began to run.

"There was some fucker spying on us," Edward said to Teresa, before quickly giving chase.

"Be careful ..." she shouted after him.

Although not as fast a runner as himself, the person in front of him was very elusive, zig-zagging like a hare being chased by a dog. For the second time that night Edward tried a rugby tackle. At the same instant the other person tried to change course. Stretching, Edward's hand just reached but slipped from a bare ankle as a splatter of sand hit him in the eyes and face. By the time Edward stood up, the other had gone.

He shouted Teresa's name. She shouted back. They made their way in the direction of each other's shouts, ending up in each other's arms.

"Who was it?" was Teresa's first question.

Edward explained what had happened. "Whoever it was was barefoot," he said, "in the frosty weather."

"The Anvy?"

"You don't believe in that old *seafóid*?"

"Who else could it be?"

"There's something very strange going on. Do you remember the night someone stuck the nettle up my arse?"

"I'm hardly likely to forget it."

"There must be some bastard jealous, trying to come between us."

"Who would want to do that?"

"My father for one maybe, he's not too keen on the match."

"I don't like it." Teresa snuggled into him, feeling a cold sweat on her back. "Do you believe in the devil?" she asked.

"I do not, and even if I did, I'm sure that that's not him. He would be the first devil anyone ever caught by the leg." He tried to reassure her jokingly. " I should have said – I'm only pulling your leg."

"Do you think he will come back?"

"He was in such a hurry to get away that I doubt it." Edward squeezed Teresa close to him. "I don't want you going out on your own at night until we get to the bottom of this."

Ω Ω Ω

"Don't move." Maggie had the hayfork to the Anvy's throat. He had been peeping into the lighted kitchen, wondering was she upstairs. She had come up behind him in the dark.

"Get in the kitchen." He stared at her, unmoving. She gave a little jab with the fork which brought it to within inches of his windpipe. He went slowly into the house, slowly backing away from her around the table. "I know who you are," she said. "Timeen Shéamais, better known around here as the

Anvy. Sit down."

She lowered the fork when he sat. "Would you like something to eat?" He just stared.

"You have nothing to fear here," Maggie said. "I'm not going to tell anyone. You can walk out that door now, and never come back, or you can call anytime for something to eat, and a chat. Nobody comes here except my sister, and she comes very seldom now that I have taken to visiting her at home since my mother died ... Would you drink a hot punch?" The Anvy didn't react, but she prepared it anyway. "I'm as much an outcast as you are,"

Maggie began, as they drank.

Ω Ω Ω

EPILOGUE

"Maggie has completely lost the block," a distraught Sarah told Tomás. "I was wondering how it is she is getting so heavy. Isn't she pregnant ..."

"Maggie?" He couldn't believe it. "But who?"

"That's the problem. She won't tell me. All she would say when I asked her was 'The Anvy.'"

Cíocras

Ar stailc ocrais atá an tAthair Peait Bairéad, mar sheasamh in aghaidh riail na hoantumha, riail is cúis le tréigean tubaisteach na sagartacha ar fud an domhain Chríostaí, dar leis.

Ardaítear buncheisteanna tábhachtacha san úrscéal seo faoi fheidhm na hEaglaise Caitlicí sa tSochaí Éireannach agus í ag druidim le deireadh na mílaoise seo; ríochtar go healaíonta agus go nádúrtha soléite ann ról an choinsiasa aonair, meaisín sofaisticiúil polaitíochta na hEaglaise—cleasaíocht neamhscrupallach Nuinteas an Phápa, cuir i gcás—nádúr an ghrá agus na collaíochta.

Lovers

Tom Connor arrives home form Dublin—he has
been lobbying the goverment to provide work
for the islanders he represents—to be told by his
housekeeper, Marion Warde, that she is pregnant
with his child. This would be a blow for any man
but it is especially disastrous because Tom is the
local parish priest. Because he is a man of strong
conscience and no believer in clerical celibacy
he determines to tell his people the truth. The
resolution of his dilemma makes for dramatic and
heartbreakingreading.

Lovers is the author's own translation of
Súil le Breith, the classic Irish-language
bestseller first published in 1983.
Bob Quinn's award-winning film,
Budawanny, was based on this novel.

*Also by Pádraig Standún
and published by Poolbeg*

Celibates

Father Pat Barrett wants to remain a priest but also wants to marry Teresa Carter and be a father to her daugthter, Jennie. He goes on hunger-stike to publicise his case, causing conflict and division in his parish and in the whole country.

Celibates is based on the author's Irish language novel *Cíocras* (Cló Iar-Chonnachta 1991)

Lovers

Tom Connor arrives home from Dublin—he has been lobbying the goverment to provide work for the islanders he represents—to be told by his housekeeper, Marion Warde, that she is pregnant with his child. This would be a blow for any man but it is especially disastrous because Tom is the local parish priest. Because he is a man of strong conscience and no believer in clerical celibacy he determines to tell his people the truth. The resolution of his dilemma makes for dramatic and heartbreaking reading.

Lovers is the author's own translation of *Súil le Breith*, the classic Irish-language bestseller first published in 1983. Bob Quinn's award-winning film, *Budawanny*, was based on this novel.